About the Author

Barbara only came to writing in her seventies when she found that she had many tales to tell about her early life and growing up as a child in an RAF family. The urge to travel was instilled into her then and she continues to follow that passion. She now lives happily at the foot of the Dandenong Ranges, in Victoria, Australia, where she writes her books and travel stories and looks forward to what her next destination has in store for her. She was once a practicing nurse and midwife but has had many other roles in her life: solo parent amongst them. She had a stroke in late 2018 which she not only survived and recovered from, but used as a springboard to begin a whole new phase in her life, in which writing has become a principal endeavour.

Never Just Anybody... Alice's Story

Barbara McCarthy

Never Just Anybody... Alice's Story

Olympia Publishers
London

www.olympiapublishers.com
OLYMPIA PAPERBACK EDITION

Copyright © Barbara McCarthy 2024

The right of Barbara McCarthy to be identified as author of
this work has been asserted in accordance with sections 77 and 78 of
the Copyright, Designs and Patents Act 1988.

All Rights Reserved

No reproduction, copy or transmission of this publication
may be made without written permission.
No paragraph of this publication may be reproduced,
copied or transmitted save with the written permission of the publisher,
or in accordance with the provisions
of the Copyright Act 1956 (as amended).

Any person who commits any unauthorised act in relation to
this publication may be liable to criminal
prosecution and civil claims for damage.

A CIP catalogue record for this title is
available from the British Library.

ISBN: 978-1-80439-836-4

This is a work of fiction.
Names, characters, places and incidents originate from the writer's
imagination, however some stories were inspired in part by real people
and events.

First Published in 2024

Olympia Publishers
Tallis House
2 Tallis Street
London
EC4Y 0AB

Printed in Great Britain

PROLOGUE

One must pause to wonder, Alice thought, *how some things come to be; why a particular path has been followed even though it has caused stumbles and pain along the way. Why me? Why now? Why then? How have I come to be here, to be who I am, doing what I do, far from where I began—with far more knowledge, though perhaps not with far more wisdom?*

She sits back in her old pink-velvet upholstered chair, so low to the ground on its curved timber legs that she has to pull herself inch by inch out of it with a frayed piece of braided rope she has tied to the round handle of her living room door. Her bare-feet rest on a small wooden stool with a soft cushion on top. She is facing away from the window, the light behind her, where the last beams from an autumn sunset relay patterns onto her walls through the open slats of the white timber-shutters.

The shadows of this season's evening remind her that her own days are also growing short, her own sunset is approaching. She imagines that she is as vital and active as she has always been—and she truly knows that her mind is sharp and her sense of humour still lingers and catches her happily off guard sometimes—but she senses that her zest for living is dimming, and knows that her energy is easily drained. She sees that her body is ageing relentlessly against its will. She has developed a tendency to list awkwardly to her right when she stands up from her chair and she often has to grab out for support to prevent herself from falling—and she loathes the insecurity and weakness she feels in that moment. Her ankles have begun to swell out of proportion to her calves, and ache most of her waking days and most of her sleepless nights. Even minor activities cause her to breathe faster, and she has to pause to recover herself.

She knows that she has much to do before her final days, when dying will take precedence over everything else and overwhelmingly sap her strength—her being—she has seen its process and its progress so many times in others' and neither welcomes nor fears it for herself. She just recognises that it is inevitable, and she cannot control its speeding advance. However, there are many things still within her control, and on her mind, and she firmly intends to act on to all of them.

She reaches over and opens the lined notebook on the small wheeled-table beside her, and pulling it towards her, she begins to write her final stories while there is energy in her, and the light is warm and good in the room around her.

Alice's thoughts are deep and sometimes troubling to her as she sifts through her mind for memories which are coloured in sepia now, or often just grey and white, and hazy too, but at the same time she knows them, remembers them, understands them. She knows that she has no peers now to talk her memories over with, to confirm the details of—no one to affirm that she is writing what was once their reality too. But she feels compelled to write her stories regardless of this—not just for the sake of telling stories, but to leave her words and her last memories to be shared. *This is now my main purpose in life*, she tells herself.

She had already compiled many stories of her early years as a legacy of her own life's truth for those she leaves behind, but then she had only written in general terms, moving quickly through her memories, not pausing on any particular decade, experience, or defining life event. She has yet to draw a complete picture of any aspect of her adult life, to show the colours and the emotions of the times she has lived through—and the people she has encountered—during the years when she was learning to be who she has been, and who she has become.

With the intense pleasure of being able to navigate herself alone through this last part of her life; to slow down, to sleep when she wants to, to go where she wants to go, and to please herself about how she presents her life-to others—and whose voice she uses—she begins to recall the first days of her long nursing career. She knows it will not be easy to tell at times, but her mind is unhampered by what she should or should not say, and she knows that her words will be honest and true. She also knows that she will not share these words with anyone until it is the complete story she wants and needs to tell, however long it takes her.

CHAPTER ONE
Welcome to St Helen's

The entrance to the nurses' home was daunting to Alice, that cold day in January; the façade was old-fashioned and imposing, the windows dark, blinds drawn like shaded eyes on either side of a tall, closed door painted in dull, dark red. The brick building was four storeys high and the prospect of entering this place made Alice shiver with dread at what may lay ahead; she had to look away, reluctant to take in any more detail. Here in her old home in suburban Melbourne—over sixty years later—the details of that entrance and her emotions as she approached it, are all crystal clear in her recall.

There was no doubt that that day was inauspicious; no amount of preparation could have equipped her for this moment she was sure, and if she had seen this place before, looked through its windows and felt its austerity, she would not have gone there. She was nineteen—soon to be twenty years of age—and was shortly to discover that she was one of the 'older ones' beginning her hospital nursing training in the England of the 1960s.

With a timid gesture Alice reached out and pressed the brass bell-push on the left of the door which was finally opened by a stern-looking, short-statured and buxom woman who asked her brusquely, 'What's your name?'. She might have hoped for a kindly 'what's your name, *dear?'* to put her at her ease, but that was not forthcoming from this person. *'I'm Alice McPhee,'* she answered quietly. The door-opener, with her round face, blue eyes and grey hair should have looked friendly and welcoming, but she did not. Without making any eye-contact the woman took one step back in her sturdy black shoes and opened the door just wide enough to let Alice pass through into the dark entrance hall with her suitcase in her hand.

Alice's father had brought her to this point—in more ways than just having driven her the fifteen miles to get there. She had a long history of uneasiness in her relationship with him, the causes of which she held steadfast in her memory and would write about much later in her life when she was seeking catharsis, but today he had merely brought her in his car, with her small brown-leather suitcase with its many pasted-on stamps from countries she had travelled to with her family, which he carried up the steep stone-steps and deposited at the entrance door. Alice—deposited like a piece of unstamped luggage herself—thanked him, and with an uncomfortable smile he told her, *'Goodbye and good luck'* and retreated down the steps back to his car before the door was opened.

Her father was in his RAF officers' blue-grey uniform and bulky winter greatcoat on this English winters' day. Sometime later when personal reflections and disclosures about this day were being shared among the young women of this new intake of student nurses, one of her groups told her she had been so very impressed that Alice's *chauffeur* had driven her there and carried her suitcase up the stairs! Her father would not have liked to be mistaken for her driver and she knew this: his status as an air force officer was a source of great pride for him.

It seemed clear to Alice on this cold morning that he was probably quite pleased to be saying farewell; there was no place for her in his house. Her presence was disruptive. She had been away from the family for over a year with her friend Jenny, working for a family in a manor house in the midlands, and then they had both travelled to Sussex, to pick apples and enjoy themselves—and revel in the social life of young people engaged in a shared activity—but her past three months at home with her family, waiting for this day, had been difficult for everyone. She had outgrown her childhood, and she had the strong feeling that she had outgrown her family in the process. She was the oldest of four children, and now there were others to take up her role as big sister and mother's helper. She had thought from time to time that to be an only child would have been a splendid thing, but she also knew that although the responsibility and burden of her role in her family was not for her any more, it had taught her many skills—practical skills—that she could take forward into her life. But she could leave home now and not be overly missed; of that she was absolutely sure.

Alice had decided that nursing was what she *must* do, having committed to it quite flippantly in the beginning by declaring to Jenny—and to anyone who asked—that nursing was what she was *filling in time for*, when she was conscientiously picking fruit on the farm. She had tossed around, and lightly considered, the prospect of other possible occupations for her to take up since leaving school when she was sixteen. She had worked in an office in London for a while until Jenny suggested they go together to take up the temporary position with the family in the manor house, but now she began to feel that the pressure was on her to '*do something really useful*' with her life. Judgement was obvious in the tone of her father's voice when he added this phrase to many of their conversations and it always sounded like one of those scolding comments that had mortified her in her early years.

She was very young—too young to make a career decision to be bonded-to forever, she thought now—but times were different then, work ethics were different, youthful aspirations were different, family expectations were different, life was different. Early marriage was always an option, of course—but this was definitely not on Alice's agenda; she had not even had a real boyfriend yet.

She had once thought that she might have a vocation to be a nun. She had observed at the convent schools she had attended the way women in long, coarse-cloth black gowns and cowls swung their rustling rosary beads from the waist—and the way they scurried along with heads bowed looking so serene and pure with their clear, scrubbed skin. The theatricality of their lives was intriguing to the young Alice. But as time went by, she became aware that not all the nuns she knew were serene women to be in awe of and aspire to follow; some were mean and tight-faced and to be feared, so the reality of living amongst such a group soon overcame any fanciful notions of a convent life and religious vocation for her.

Alice took a job in a large department store in London (another career she soon knew she would not ever want to pursue) to earn enough money for the shoes and books she had been told to bring with her on her first day at St Helen's. *Shoes?* Well, not the attractive, low-heeled, patent-leather variety she had become used to wearing in her teens—instead these were practical and sturdy brown-leather shoes, laced high up on the arch, with chunky stacks for heels and worn with thick denier, beige stockings—without the delightful seams at the back which she usually wore just like every fashionable young woman of the day. Later, much later, she would become proud of her whole uniform—and amazingly also rather proud of her shoes, although when she bought them from the shop in London that was on the list she had been sent, she wasn't very pleased—and not looking forward to wearing-them-in either.

The other items that made up the hospital uniform at St Helen's were described to them at their orientation gathering on that first day, in the cold library on the ground floor of the nurses' home where the stern door-opener of earlier in the day addressed them: 'You must not go outside the hospital in your uniform without permission—you must change into mufti,' she announced, standing with her arms folded akimbo, leaning back and rocking on her heels like a short, round-bodied army sergeant, as she continued her instructions—'your uniform must always be clean and your apron changed at each shift.' She didn't say to them 'you should shower or bath every day, too', which is just as well, because they didn't do that than in the England as Alice knew—*'top and tail'* they did daily though, in front of a basin of warm water with a cotton flannel and a bar of brown Pear's soap or creamy Imperial Leather (if they were lucky enough to have it). Hair-washing was not a regular event either, once a week seemed to suffice in those days. Perhaps this was because of the temperament of the English climate or perhaps because of the rarity of bathroom facilities in homes, but that is how it was. 'However,' their instructor continued, 'your shoes must be cleaned every day.' They were being told in no uncertain terms what was expected of them. Alice was familiar with the shoe-cleaning chore; children in her family were taught well— 'If your shoes are shabby, it will reflect the person you are, and people will notice if you don't take care of them,' they were told repeatedly by their father. Their mother had no such affectations but she never commented; she didn't contradict her husband often, and certainly not when he was being firm about his protocols.

'And your caps must be securely attached with bobby-pins, and your hair must be above your collar and tied back from your face,' their trainer intoned to the bemused group. Many of them had long hair 'teased' to make it look higher and fuller in the fashion of the day (after it was cried on big rollers under an electric contraption that blew warm air into a plastic hood placed over the head), and they each knew without doubt that this hair advice was aimed at them personally. They listened intently to the talk but no one took notes; they knew they would remember her words to them for ever and ever and a day. 'And in your uniform pocket you should carry a tin of Atrixo hand cream—you will find that your hands become quite dry after all the hand-washing.' Her last instruction was delivered with a wry, closed-lip and knowing smile, full of warning that made it clear that hand-washing must be paramount in their work-a-day lives. And indeed, it was, as they discovered.

Later when they gathered together in a 'get-to know-you' session, most of them still bemused, some amused and some quite perplexed by this introduction to St Helen's—they admitted to each other that the words that had resonated from the introductory speech were 'mufti' (what on earth was that?), and Atrixo hand cream? Oh… and the warning that 'the nurses'-home doors will be locked at ten thirty p.m. every night without fail,' so 'woe betide you if you are late coming in—the home-sister will catch you', was clearly recalled and raised quite a few concerns and much discussion.

Alice knew what *mufti* meant, coming from a military family, and she understood the significance of uniform in a structured life—giving a sense of belonging to a group, a tribe, a cohort—and the locking of the door wasn't of any concern to her then, but she wasn't totally sure if this life with all its apparent rigidity was going to be right for her, and she had a disturbing sense of foreboding that stayed with her for the remainder of the day.

She went to bed that night in the little room assigned to her on the second floor, with her name handwritten on a card inside a metal bracket on the door. She was anxious in this strange place and in a strange bed with its cotton multi-coloured counterpane and one woollen blanket for comfort. The room was warmed by an old noisy cream-painted panelled radiator under the window and Alice could see tall trees somewhere in the distance and brick walls on each side with many windows just like hers.

She had brought very little with her—her warm woollen coat in the style that Julie Christie wore as Lara in *Dr Zhivago* which Alice loved to wear with her black knee-high boots, and she had brought skirts and jumpers, shoes, and her few friendly and familiar books that she unpacked from her suitcase—before storing it in the top of the narrow wardrobe. She had just three volumes of *Readers Digest novels*, (condensed versions) which had coloured ribbons attached to the spines for page-saving. They looked pathetically minimal on the little bookshelf beside her three newly purchased text books; one on anatomy and physiology, one on medical conditions (with horrifyingly explicit photographs she had noted) and the third one was a small red nurses' dictionary. Later she would add a single volume text on general-surgery to the shelf—and later still books on the travels she dreamed of taking in Africa and Asia, and paperbacks of her favourite novels, '*The Father Brown Stories*', H. Ryder Haggard's '*She*', and '*Gone with the Wind*'. She finally placed her small transistor radio which had been a constant source of comfort and a companion to her throughout her adolescence, on the desk beside the bed. And here she was—unpacked and ready to start a new, grown-up phase in her life.

She was sad that night, but she had no tears to shed, and she dare not anyway because she was sure her face would show that she had been crying when they all met in the ground-floor sitting-room the next day. She was not ever one of those lucky people who could shed a tear and wipe it away quickly so no one saw her weakness (like her heroines of her films and novels were able to do); no, for Alice, her heart was on her sleeve, and her face clearly showed her emotions which were close to the brim always, she was too easily moved to tears—as she was for most of her life as it turned out—and particularly so when she was anxious and feeling out of her depth, as she was on that first night at St Helens. So, in front of her wall mirror she prepared for her debut as a student nurse—she rolled her self-blonded, shoulder length hair (which she dampened with warm water from the wash-basin in the corner of the room), onto spikey rollers (no soft Velcro rollers then) and went to bed with her little red travel alarm-clock set for six a.m. on the desk beside her.

The following morning a large box was delivered to her room which contained two starched and carefully folded green-striped dresses (short sleeved, without collars), two stiff white strips in the shape of collars, two larger flat pieces of starched white material, an adjustable belt of the same colour and stripe as the cotton dresses, and a brown paper packet of white buttons and small steel clips.

There was probably no real planning, no clever design to get the group together and help them 'bond'—that was a term not used in a psychological sense in the 1960s, it was only used with reference to gluing two things together—but as they started to put their heads out of their doors looking for enlightenment about what to do with the buttons and clips in the box, there was a spark of connection between them—a sense of, *'we're all in the same boat'*, followed by a genuine sharing of knowledge and mutual kindness between them. The more nimble-fingered among them helped clip buttons to the caps and belts but they were all dismayed to find that this tedious chore had to be done at every dress and cap change. Uniforms would be laundered for them and returned within a couple of days, they had been told, and this was happy news—no washing, starching and ironing to be done, thank goodness! All their meals were provided but they would only receive ten pound *a month* stipend (pocket-money really) after board and lodging had been taken out. This was a sobering thought for most of them. Alice had earned ten pound *a week* when she worked in the office, and also for her Christmas work in the department store, and even after paying rent money at home she always seemed to have enough left over for herself. Her student nurse 'wage' seemed like a very paltry sum to her—but she would have to learn to make do.

Information was the key to personal success and survival in those early days at St Helen's. It was important to know where to find a seat in the dining-room (and at what times), what tables to avoid (ward sisters sat on one table near the window, tutoring-staff on another, and midwives on yet another, and each of these groups had their own sitting room so that there was no mingling of the hierarchy); and it was important to know whom to speak to—and when—in order to avoid a humiliating, and often public, dressing-down. It soon became clear that they should all 'toe-the-line' or they would not be well accepted and they would be brought before matron to be dealt with.

Alice was in trepidation about the threat of a matronly reprimand. She didn't take to scolding, or criticism, very well;

she never had and never would. When she was a child, she had resorted to humiliating tears if she had been told-off, whether the reprimand was justified or not. She didn't learn to speak up, to stand up for herself, until she was much older, and even then, she would become emotional at any expression of disapproval. She kept her personal resentments and hurts to herself for most of her life. Her convent school education, in her early years, had exposed her to nuns who, despite their humble mystique, were strong on physical, and verbal, discipline, and they used their little black sticks without hesitation. The thought of this hospital matron, and the threat of her punishment, put Alice in mind of those past experiences with unpleasant clarity.

When she was working over the Christmas season in the department store, she had been upset by a fellow worker, an older woman who had worked in the gift-department for many years, who spoke to her roughly and gave her orders constantly. One day Alice made the chastening mistake of speaking to the female floor-manager about how she felt, and was firmly told to dry her tears and get over it. 'Things will be worse for you in nursing,' she told her. Alice began to think that she might have been right about that, and perhaps she should have taken heed and considered another occupation!

Alice had always found making friends fraught with anxieties. The constant moving to new postings in her young life, being the new girl at school, always in a uniform that didn't match with that of her new classmates which set her apart and made her stand out, but that was only part of the problem for her. Every school she arrived at had a different curriculum and she was sometimes behind the rest of the class and had to work hard to catch up. At her first grammar school, as a thirteen-year-old, she travelled by bus, once a week during school hours and just after lunch (a proper sit-down meal was always served at school in those days), to visit a retired tutor who was to bring her up to the expected standard in French language. Of course, this meant that she missed out on some other subject which was usually sport or gym or music which she thought she might have preferred, but the extra French tuition stuck with her, and she was always happy that she had that in her background, along with Latin which was much easier for her to learn and was to come in very handy for understanding medical terminology. Her general knowledge was good too, but it was a long time before she had enough courage to put her hand up in class to answer a question in any of the many new-school environments she encountered.

It was hard for her to find a niche in a group that had already formed its friendship circles at the beginning of term, because she always joined a new school mid-term, and never at the beginning of a school year. Although they were all starting at the same time, in the same intake, at St Helen's, the prospect of finding a friend amongst the disparate group she had seen around her that first day, did bother her a great deal. She didn't think in terms of finding 'friends', as in more than one—she would be quite happy with just one friend, she thought, someone she hoped would understand her, someone she could understand and confide in. That would be nice. She could only see one person who she thought might be that one—Pauline, who later told her that she thought Alice's father was her chauffeur dropping her off on that first day, seemed to have a good sense of humour which Alice liked. But none of this was an immediate priority for her—and as it turned out Pauline was not to be the friend she was hoping for—now she had to get dressed up in her uniform, and look as if she belonged in the group; just for once she was at the beginning of something, however it all turned out.

After breakfast in the main dining-room, where they were subtly inspected by the senior students sitting at their own tables in their own groups, they were led around the nurses' home by the home-sister, at quick marching pace. They followed her like a clutch of baby ducklings in single file—each of them wearing stiff, starched collars that grazed the back of the neck (and later needed Atrixo to soothe) and with caps flapping on their nodding heads, they completed the tour. It would be some weeks before the skill of securing a stiffly-starched cap on a head of teased hair would be confidently accomplished by them all, and they spent a great deal of time practising the art.

In the front entrance of the nurses' home, the home-sister's office was pointed out to them, along with a list of the home-sister's responsibilities which included, they were reminded, locking the doors at ten thirty p.m. And, once again the discipline meted out to anyone breaking the rules was re-enforced. They certainly got the message about that in those early days, but many would flout the rules in the years to follow and discovered that there was indeed access to the nurses' home after hours through the casualty department doors and, if you were discreet, you would go unnoticed! But if you didn't want to risk being caught, it was easier to stay out all night they found out—and many did do just that!

Among the features shown to them on their tour was a wall of little boxes—pigeon-holes—labelled in alphabetical order, where letters from families and friends could be found. No visitors were encouraged inside the nurses' home, they could be met at the front door and taken into the students' sitting room for a short visit. Alice would rarely have visitors during her training years, but she did receive thin blue airmail-letters from her mother, written with black biro in her beautiful flowing script, after her family had moved to Australia during Alice's second year at St Helens. Occasionally there were very welcome insightful and philosophical letters in her pigeon-hole, sent by her old teacher from her convent school days in the Middle East, and much later, in her third year, there were love letters and poems from an interesting young man called Phillip, with whom Alice fell in love. His letters, on blue Basildon Bond unlined paper and matching envelope were all written with fountain pen and ink, and were a thrilling find under the pile of mail for students with surnames beginning with the same letter as Alice's. She eventually made a good friend in her group through these pigeon-holes. They both shared the same box, and Alice found a letter addressed to Monica amongst her own. It was from her mother, Monica told her. As Alice handed it to her, she remarked that the handwriting was 'forthright'. There was something in this light exchange that seemed encouraging to Monica, and some weeks later when she and Alice became friends, she reminded her about it and they both laughed. '*Forthright*', seemed such an old-fashioned word for a young student nurse to say then, but Alice had many words in her head from her early family life and travels, from listening to her father and from her own reading, that she seldom had a chance to speak aloud. However, as it turned out when she finally met Monica's mother, she didn't find her *forthright* at all; just a rather vacuous and childishly-manipulative little woman. But that meeting lay ahead in another time and after much had happened in their lives.

CHAPTER TWO
Learning to Care

Given that information was key, and prior knowledge would stand you in good stead in this new world, it was clear to Alice quite early on that she was on the backfoot as far as knowledge of hospitals was concerned. Her only experiences had been her own tonsils and adenoids operation ('Ts and As', as they learnt to say), when she was seven years old, and a brief visit to see her little sister who was hospitalised with a chest infection, when they lived overseas. The only other time she had entered into a hospital was one day after fruit-picking had finished when she went with Jenny to see someone who had had their appendix removed. They were late arriving for visiting hour that afternoon, and got there just in time to see a nurse in a white apron and a stiff white veil clang a large bell at the ward-door announcing that everyone had to leave; visiting hour was over. So, for all intents and purposes Alice was a 'blank canvas', an innocent in the system and unaware of the procedures of hospital life and actually no idea what went on behind closed doors on the ward after visiting hour was over. But she was soon to find out.

Preliminary Training School (PTS) began within a day, and the eighteen newly arrived young women (no men—it was unheard of that a man could be a nurse at that time although that was about to change), read in their '*Welcome to St Helens*' typed notes that they were to assemble at the nursing-school, in the grounds of the hospital, to meet the tutoring staff at eight forty-five a.m. precisely. The tutors would prepare them for what to expect when they were on the wards for the first time, they read, and they were to wear their uniforms and bring their aprons, fob-watches, and hand cream with them.

Alice started to have a little fun, and her anxiety was lifting. The group laughed together—and at each other—when they were learning the basics of a nurse's duties like flicking mercury down inside a glass thermometer before placing it carefully under the patient's tongue. They soon learned that flicking too hard resulted in these fragile instruments dropping out of a hand with disastrous consequences. Spilled mercury was almost impossible to pick up from the floor and rolled away from them in tiny silver balls. There were a great many things to share and laugh at in these early days of training.

They each spent a vast amount of time taking and recording TPRs and BP's (pulse, temperature, blood pressure and respirations were not referred to as 'vital signs' in those days). Using their fob-watches to time them, they meticulously counted breaths while trying not to let the patient know the rise and fall of their chest was being observed! The patients that had been selected for them to practice on were so helpful and took it all quite seriously, which was a nice confidence builder for everyone and made those early learning times on the wards a pleasure. All details had to be accurately recorded on the patients' charts under the guidance of the clinical tutors, checking and checking again that they had correctly seen the top of the mercury when it had risen in the glass-tube of the thermometer to give them a temperature measurement. It seemed so difficult at first but after a very short time it just became an automatic routine. When electronic thermometers, blood pressure and heart monitors came to be medical tools-of-choice a few decades later, Alice could only marvel at the simplicity and time-saving convenience of these inventions although she often missed the old ways. Many chores in hospitals in those early days were very time-consuming, impractical and cumbersome, and so many of them were the responsibilities of the student nurses, and they had to learn to work with them efficiently. However, Alice always thought that counting a pulse at a wrist with gentle fingers feeling the beat of the artery against the bone and tendon, was a very valuable way to assess a patient. It wasn't just the rate of the beat but also the strength and tension and regularity of it, and also the way a patient responded to the nurse's touch which said so much about their state of mind.

Alice's guide and mentor whom she admired and looked up in her last years at school was Sister Helen who was both a teacher and a nun, and to her surprise and delight she could see her same admirable qualities in St Helen's senior nurse tutor, Miss Bronsen. She was wise, encouraging, knowledgeable, kind, loved her subject and was proud to be a nurse. She was also an excellent teacher. She wore a grey-linen dress with long sleeves which she rolled up into little white frilled and elasticated cuffs so that her forearms were free of everything, including rings and watches (rings and other jewellery were not allowed to be worn on duty, they had been told). And when she was with her students on the ward her fob-watch was pinned to the left side of her dress where she also wore just a single state registration badge, and her students learnt to pin their watches to the left side of their starched aprons too, under their name badges (no first names), so they could clearly read the seconds ticking by when they were taking a pulse or checking respirations. Miss Bronsen also wore a stiff, white detachable collar like theirs, which must have scratched her neck just like Alice's did, and her hemline reached respectably below her knees too, as was expected. She wore the same laced leather shoes, but in black, and also the thick stockings of her students, but she wore a frilled cap which set her apart in the hierarchy of nurses at St Helens. Alice didn't know then that she would aspire to be just like her, and many years later, half way across the world, she became a midwifery tutor, hoping to inspire her students to be caring and thoughtful too, although by this time her uniform was a white permanent-press dress without a belt, with navy-blue epaulettes attached to the shoulders with press-studs. She would also wear a frilled cap with this uniform—until caps were phased out for nurses because they were deemed to be 'unhygienic and impractical'. All those years ago, the nurse's cap seemed such a lovely thing to wear, and Alice saw it as a symbol of skill, kindness and caring—and of what nursing came to mean to her, really.

Classroom teaching in nursing hadn't evolved to 'student participation' or 'self-directed learning' in the mid-1960s. The notion of preparing a presentation to be shared in class, using butchers' paper and felt-tip pens was so novel that when it was introduced at the end of Alice's third year of training, it seemed to be an enormously scary innovation. It was bad enough to have to stand up and answer questions in class out loud, but to be in front of a class, sharing your personal views and ideas, and knowing that your drawings were not very good, was terrifying. It was far more comfortable to be behind a desk, listen to a lecture and write your answers to a list of questions written on the blackboard, then go to your room, in privacy, to revise what you had been told. Alice was reticent in many situations, and a classroom was one of them. It would be many years before she overcame this, and she was always sensitive to the needs of her less-confident midwifery students because of her own early experiences. She was so uncertain of what was expected of her, and how she should behave, during these early days, and her lack of confidence in herself, her lack of self-esteem and self-worth, was very apparent to her, and must have been blindingly clear to her peers, her superiors and her tutors.

Fledgling student nurses were expected to do many menial tasks, some of them quite trivial; later many of these tasks would be thought of as 'demeaning' duties when nursing moved into university and 'nurse training' became an undergraduate degree course. But in the days when Alice was in hospital training it was just what they did, and they just did what was expected of them, and these lowly tasks became part and parcel of their job and their working lives.

Alice had tortuous difficulty with simple protocols on occasion—never wanting to do the wrong thing at any time which was such a throwback to the times that she was reprimanded for doing the wrong thing in her childhood, something she came to understand and learned to overcome. *Should she take her shoes off to stand on a chair when replacing the freshly-laundered cotton privacy curtains around a patient's bed?* This was just one such dilemma for her in the beginning, but the safety risks of standing on a chair to do this never entered her mind at all! She never knew whether she should knock on the ward sister's door when she could see through the glass that she was only reading a novel, or should she quietly go away and wait till the door was open? So many other early insecurities went with Alice into nursing, and then even beyond that: there were too many to confront and understand the origin of until quite late in her life—but that all belongs in another story. She eventually came to terms with many of her insecurities, although she never hardened to reprimands, scolding and criticism in her life. She did, however, come to learn that she had emotional intelligence, empathy and conscientiousness—qualities that made her stay on duty long after her shift had ended to help the staff or to comfort a patient, and later to support a mother in labour. But in those early days of her nursing career, she was tormented by her self-doubt and feelings of inadequacy.

Alice soon settled into the PTS routine of class lectures, ward instruction with the clinical teachers who supervised their 'one on one' patient care—and eating! Breakfast, lunch, and an evening meal, with fresh baked biscuits and fruit cake on offer for morning and afternoon teas in between, was all in the order of the day, enjoyed in the convivial company of her group, and very much looked forward to. Inevitably she began to put on weight, like most of the group did. Then, almost in the nick of time, the weeks of PTS were over and reality took its place, and the extra weight just dropped off—thanks to long days and hard physical work!

Early shift—a seven a.m. start—wrapped in her black woollen cape racing to her first assigned ward—the children's ward—no familiar faces from her group to share a smile or joke with, instead there she was, standing too long in the ward-sister's office, while the night-staff reported their handover on each child to the incoming day-staff, and Alice fainted to the floor, for the first time in her life. She noted that the sister-in-charge had forgotten to put blue eyeshadow on her right eyelid that morning, before she slid into her faint. Sister ordered someone to fetch Alice a glass of water and dismissed the other day-staff to go and start their shift by first reading the ward-duties book to see what tasks and patients they were assigned and which meal break they were to attend. Alice was duly sent to join them as soon as she was up on her feet again, pale but stoic and watching the clock for morning tea time.

It seemed that nothing she did would ever please this ward-sister (nor the sister-in-charge on her next ward either, she found to her dismay). She took this very much to heart at the time but later she came to understand that she was being tried and pushed and she was an easy target too, and in actual fact her ward reports were always very good and complimentary about her skills and her attitude. There was an exception to her good reports just once, on the TB ward (tuberculosis, a word Alice scrambled her pronunciation of always, putting the emphasis on the wrong syllable for no reason she could understand). She was in her third year at St Helen's before she started on this ward rotation, and she was burning the candle at both ends at the time—and not just with study!

On her first ward experience, with all the sick children and their treatments, she learnt the hard lessons of how she was expected to behave as a nurse. She had a great deal of experience with children, coming as she did from a family where she was the oldest daughter, and she knew how to distract them, engage them and entertain them. One day after lunch, she sat on the bed of a little boy who had Paget's disease (a severe form of bone deformity), playing cards with him. His hips were in plaster of Paris and his legs were outstretched in traction with a complicated design of pulleys and weights, and he often became frustrated with being so severely restrained—as any eight-year-old would be. Alice thought that a game of 'Snap!' with some coloured cards might be a nice thing to do and would cheer him up. Suddenly there was a loud rapping on the corridor window and there was sister on the other side gesticulating and shouting, *'Get OFF that bed... and go and do something useful, nurse!'* Alice learned about the adrenalin reaction of 'flight and fright' that afternoon! And she never sat on a patient's bed again until she became a midwife over fifteen years later. Sitting on a bed of a woman in labour, feeling contractions with her hand, noting their strength and counting their frequency with her watch, was always easy and natural for her. It was usually quite comforting for the mother too and better than having someone stooping over beside the bed, Alice always thought. Sadly, even this became almost an obsolete practice when electronic labour-monitors took over. Alice was often to lament the downside of technical progress in her career.

There were many sights, procedures and illnesses that confronted the new students in the wards for the first time, and as the group became more connected, they shared their experiences, talking and laughing about them, and often crying about them too.

When a ten-year-old boy died from kidney-failure on her first ward, Alice was distraught. There was no 'de-briefing' or counselling to help her in this situation. She had been there when he had painful treatments performed—handing the instruments to the doctor to insert into this poor child's body to get fluids and tissue samples none of which were going to prolong his life, or relieve his suffering—and she watched as his little body ballooned out of all proportion to his height, becoming stiff with the fluid accumulating in his arms and legs, and when she washed him in his bed she noted that he had a body-smell like bleach. She saw how he deteriorated day by day until he lost consciousness slipping into nothingness with his parents beside him.

She was to see death in many forms and at many stages of life during her nursing career, but the death of the very young, the death of a newborn baby or a stillbirth, were the deaths that she recalled with emotion every time, tears welling up in her eyes. She railed against the waste of the potential of a life over too soon. She resolved very early in her career that she would always treat death well, and treat it kindly, and give support to the people left behind. She would often choose to sit with the dying who had no one with them, until it was clear that they needed to be alone to give themselves permission to die.

She embraced death and caring for the dying as much as she embraced caring for and looking after the living, and all the patients that she had the honour to nurse. With the exception of the patients who, often through no fault of their own, became abusive and difficult to manage and would scream and shout all night in a demented state, disturbing the ward and the other patients, to her chagrin! She came to learn that for the most part these psychotic episodes could be managed with some humour— when all else failed.

On one evening shift Alice could hear a woman screaming in a loud cockney accent in her room in the corridor away from the main ward, '*Let me orf this train*!' In her confused state of mind this poor woman was convinced that the rails on her bed, which were keeping her safe from falling out, were the rails of the Blackheath to London trainline. Alice stayed with her and comforted her for a while and when the woman asked her suspiciously what her name was. ('*oo the 'ell are you*?' she actually demanded to know), Alice, who tried to be respectful to all her patients, told her her name. This was a major mistake she soon found out. As she left the room the woman had replaced '*Let me orf this train*!' with '*Nurse McPhee, Nurse McPhee*' over and over again for hours and hours, in a loud and mocking tone! There were many things to learn the hard way it seemed!

Confusion in the elderly in hospital has always been

recognised as a common manifestation of being in an unfamiliar place, Alice learnt, and was often a result of medications and could occur after an anaesthetic particularly, but the best treatment then was considered to be chemical and physical restraint. Paraldehyde with its strong and pervasive smell of acetic acid that lasted for many hours in the air, and on uniforms, was administered by a doctor as an injection into the buttock while the patient was restrained by the nurses, and then very often canvas jackets were wrapped around the patient's torso and tied firmly under the bed base—a practice that was abandoned in later years. Paraldehyde was a standard treatment for confused patients, and was also considered to be very effective as a sedative for out-of-control epileptics at the time, despite its known side-effects. There was no need to find a glass syringe to draw it up into either (it was known to react with plastic and rubber), most of the syringes in use in the mid-1960s were glass and were either disinfected by immersing them in the boiling water of the steam steriliser in the clinical room and then leaving them to dry on a steel rack, or sending them to be wrapped in cloth and autoclaved with the operating theatre's instruments. Alice went on to nurse long after this time and long enough to see disposable, heavily-polluting plastic as the material of choice in the manufacture of so many items that in her early days would be cleaned and sterilised and then re-used.

All the wards in St Helens main block were organised into one long ward and a couple of four-bed rooms and single rooms in the corridor which connected the wards through swing doors. The single rooms were used for infectious patients or those needing terminal or special care, and the long 'Nightingale' wards had beds facing each other, eight on each side, with windows between them and trestle tables in the middle where lunches could be served to ambulant and recovering patients. A heated, wheeled-trolley was brought from the main hospital kitchen and food was served out onto plates by ward auxiliaries and supervised by the sister-in-charge in the kitchen with its gleaming stainless-steel benches and sinks. Each individual tray was taken to the bedside by a nurse who stayed to help the patient sit up or to cut up their food for them, if they didn't need feeding that is (there were no troublesome plastic packets to open then), and the nurse would place a linen table napkin over the bedsheets and place the call bell close by in case they needed it just as they had been taught to do in PTS, all very orderly and precise. Civilised actually, Alice thought. There was very little wastage of food on the ward because each plate was personally prepared by the nurse-in-charge with quantities just right for each patient depending on their condition and dietary needs. '*Healthy and wholesome*', was how Alice described the patients' food to her mother when she went home for a visit sometime after starting on the wards.

Alice was full of stories about her first days as a nurse-in-training, and her mother listened with great interest as she busied herself in the kitchen baking for her family while Alice washed the dishes and set the table. Alice was always a helper, not just a mother's helper at home but it was also what she did throughout her life when she was to be a caring advocate in many of the positions that she held. Perhaps Mother showed just a hint of envy, Alice thought to herself later on the bus ride back to the hospital, that she not only had a career ahead of her but that she was so excited by it. And Alice felt happy about where she was in her life at that time and she knew that she would never be a stay-at-home mother if she ever got married and had children

Those early days at St Helen's were full and tiring for

everyone—so much to see and do and make sense of. By the time of their first study block, six weeks after the end of PTS Alice had questions leaping through her head and disturbing her sleep. Some of the group found it hard to come to terms with all the stressful input about this stage. For some their English language skills were inadequate for them to cope, so they dropped out and went home, but these were in the minority and they had come from countries that did not prepare them for England and the English way of life. 'Natural attrition', they called it. Clearly nursing was not, and never was, for everyone but Alice, and those she had got to know best, stayed until the end; or nearly to the end. Alice was to leave three weeks short of the end of her fourth year as it turned out and she never was awarded the hospital badge that she had earned. This early departure was to become a pattern in Alice's life, which had begun with her perpetual moves to new postings with her service family, and it was this moving on, moving past, flying away and embracing change always, which eventually led to her writing her life story to help her make sense of it all, in the broader context of having lived a full life.

This was Beatlemania time, not many years after the assassination of JFK, when bush fires raged in Tasmania, and the death penalty was finally abolished in Britain, but Alice missed much of this tumultuous and eventful time—she was engrossed in forming new ideas, learning new skills, absorbing everything around her, while still knowing that she had much more to learn.

She was troubled sometimes but still aware that she was where she wanted to be. She wasn't homesick or yearning for any other life than the one she had just then, but she was thoughtful and disturbed by her nightly dreams and acutely aware that her family would soon be leaving for Australia. She remembered stories Sister Helen had told her wide-eyed and attentive pupils about how she had left her little Italian village in her mid-teens on a bus to Naples to begin her novitiate as a nun. The nun had tears in her eyes when she told the class her story and she recalled the memory of saying goodbye to her family that she didn't see again for twenty years. Alice was moved to tears too at the time, and although she had none of those sad feelings of separation that Sister Helen had talked about, the parallels between entering a convent and learning to be a nun and a teacher, and Alice starting her nursing training, was not lost on her although she never saw herself as being in a vocation in any religious sense.

Patients stayed for quite a long time in hospital for most conditions: overnight stays were almost unheard of; 'keyhole surgery' for gallbladder removal for instance, which meant that minimal time was spent in hospital, was far away into the future. Medical treatments for skin conditions were often lengthy affairs too, involving long hospital stays with daily baths for blistering skins such as that which occurs in life-threatening pemphigus vulgaris. Although steroid treatments were available, simple herbal-soaks were still in use and patients had to be wheeled to a special bathroom near to the medical ward, and lowered into healing baths. There were very few mechanical aids; even primitive aids like hoists and canvas slings were not always available and so, more often than not, two people, one on each side taking an arm, would swing the patient into and out of a bath—it was quicker and easier in a busy day, and there were no manual-lifting rules in place to stop the practice. Nor were there weight-lifting rules; all patients were moved up the bed or raised up to place a bedpan underneath them by shoulder lifts (they called it the *Australian lift*) and with practice, even two nurses of disparate heights could still manage this manoeuvre—when it was well coordinated to preserve vulnerable backs.

Nurses gave complete patient care in Alice's training days—from shaving skin sites in preparation for surgery to cleaning bedside lockers and daily 'damp-dusting' of all ward surfaces around the beds. They washed the hair of the bedridden too—using a stainless-steel bowl at the head of the bed and red rubber mackintoshes to protect the bed sheets, and they soon became proficient in this—to the point where Alice began to think she could have been a hairdresser! Bedmaking was always the nurses' responsibility, and as new students they were carefully instructed on how to work in pairs, folding back the bed cover three times, then the blankets and finally the sheets, onto a straight-back chair precisely placed at the end of the bed. Precision was the order of the day—and efficiency, and no wastage of clean bed sheets either—they were only changed when really necessary. Working in unison, they created perfect corners, mirroring each other in their system so that one of the pair didn't get ahead of the other. When all the beds were made on the ward they could look back and see the pristine order they had left behind with top sheets turned back eighteen inches over the coloured cotton bedspread which matched the other beds, and all the pillows placed with the open end of the pillow-cases facing away from the ward door. It seemed so overly fastidious to the new students at the start, but then they absorbed the routine and its peculiarities into their being with such passion that even when nursing became more relaxed in these matters, Alice still made her beds in much the same fashion.

CHAPTER THREE
Making Friends—and Stories to Tell

In the first days of starting their training, they looked each other over, weighed each other up as potential friends or just colleagues, watched their reactions to the stories that the more senior students told of their nursing experiences and, with no rush whatsoever, started to make friendly connections.

One story that was spread around in the nurses sitting room by the students from the previous intake who had firsthand knowledge, was of a potentially tragic accident that happened just before Alice started at St Helens when a car drove through an iron-spiked fence surrounding a local park and impaled the driver through the chest before landing in the lake. The young woman driver was brought to the casualty department with a spike '*in-situ*' (another brand-new term to learn) and the surgeons removed it with extreme difficulty and expertise, and she lived.

Casualty departments became 'Accident and Emergency' and then just 'Emergency' over the years, but casualty at St Helen's in the 1960s dealt with all the trauma, car accidents and walk in complaints that modern Emergency department's deal with—and with only quite basic equipment and minimal staffing to boot, but they didn't have the added complexity of drug and alcohol abuse to the same degree. It was never suggested that the young driver had been under the influence of alcohol at the time of her accident, and she wouldn't have been tested either.

Jharma from India, and Lian who came from Hong Kong, were as enthralled by the story of the girl in the lake as Alice was, and they became her first friends from their group. When they walked together to the local public library in their precious time off, they would stop at the lake near the repaired iron fence and imagine just how awful the experience must have been for everyone concerned, including the nurses on duty in casualty that day, and Alice hoped to goodness that she would never see anything so bad. Of course, she did see bad things; many bad things—that was inevitable, and although witnessing many traumatic events in her career this first story never left her. She often wondered about the effects that this accident would have had on the young woman victim, physically and psychologically, but they never learnt anything more about the outcome of this event.

Jharma told them stories of how she came to St Helen's, which captivated Alice's imagination in their honesty and description. She knew that there was no exaggeration in her story that on her flight over to London on her way to St Helens, Jharma had watched how the other passengers used their knives and forks and she imitated them. In her Indian culture they used their right hand to transfer food to the mouth and Alice knew this from observation when she had lived in the Middle East with her family. Jharma's older sister had trained at the same hospital a few years before, and was very British in her ways, if not in her sleek, dark looks, and she went on to marry a London business man and raise a family in Surrey. Lian, on the other hand, was less confident in her place in British society. Although Hong Kong was still part of the British Empire in the sixties and had adopted many British customs—as had India—the Chinese cultural influence was strong in Lian who had been born to a family that lived a simple life away from a big city. Lian was the only child in her Chinese family although the times of a one-child policy had not yet been implemented those days were coming. But Lian was comfortable with the knowledge that her family had sent her to England to have a better life and she intended to pursue that goal to please her family, even if she never returned to see them. There were so many things to talk about, many things about the world and its people to understand; Alice asked questions and listened carefully to the answers and stored them away in her imagination for another day. She was continually amazed at how soon her new friends assimilated to the hospital— and the English way of life, which Alice took for granted having her origins in British culture, and she marvelled at how they accepted the vagaries of a climate so unlike what they had known. Alice spent a lot of her off-duty time with these interesting companions in those initial days.

The first study-block was a welcome relief after early shift starts, long working days, and split-shifts, which gave them a three-hour break in the afternoon and then back on duty until ten p.m. before handing over to the night-staff. Night duty was to come a little later in the year for her group, and then they were rostered on for just a few weeks at a time, with their numbers staggered, so that there were not too many inexperienced students working in the night-hours at the same time. When it was Alice's turn, she had a pretty good idea of what to expect and how to cope, she had listened well to many night-staff handovers, but she was still shocked at the amount of work that was expected of them during the night hours—and she was alarmed by the intimidating and dreaded authority exerted by the night sisters-in-charge who supervised the hospital.

If she had thought at first that the hospital matron might have been an unnerving person to encounter, she hadn't yet learned the effect of hearing the swing doors between the wards pushed open and the appearance of the night-sister striding down the corridor. Alice's day-duty experiences on the ward were replicated on nights, and she never seemed to get anything right for one particular night sister and she was timid in her presence and dreaded her arrival on the ward. *'Well, nurse! Are his pupils dilated or not? Answer me!'* For the life of her Alice couldn't work out the difference between dilated and constricted when confronted in this way and with legs like jelly, standing before her tormenter, she wondered how long she would last on night duty—or in nursing at all actually—if she couldn't cope with this haranguing.

Just two night-sisters supervised the entire hospital, so with all their time pressures they would quickly march the junior students along the ward expecting to have a report on each patient, inspect the night report for Matron to peruse later—the report was hand written by the nurse-in-charge (a staff-nurse usually or sometimes a third-year student), about the most seriously ill patients—and then she would be on her way. That is until she had to be called back to check a DDA (drugs administered under the Dangerous Drug Act) which were kept under lock and key and only night-sisters and staff nurses had access to them with their own keys. Heroin was still used quite frequently for pain then, and was reputed to be an excellent narcotic analgesic given as an injection under the skin on the upper arm. The patients' most likely to be in need of strong pain relief were often greatly emaciated due to advanced cancers, and Alice knew that her injections hurt them, but seeing the peaceful reprieve that the drug gave made it just bearable for her to administer.

While there was caution practiced in the storing and administration of DDAs—names and signatures carefully entered into a big book in the clinical room near the drug cupboard—there was a lax attitude towards many other medications. One nurse would take a trolley with the tray of night sedations in little glass bottles, a jug of warm milk for a cup of Horlicks or Milo served in a plastic beaker, from bed to bed around the ward, and rarely would a warm drink—or a sleeping tablet—be refused. Long wards could be busy and noisy overnight and patients would be disturbed when someone else was wheeled in as an admission—or wheeled out to the mortuary—and a little yellow or blue tablet helped with sleep. They also helped night nurses' sleep during the day, and as these barbiturates were not double-checked or counted, or even entered on patients charts in those days, it was not uncommon for a couple of pills to be popped into a uniform pocket beside the pair of round-ended scissors and the useful tin of Atrixo, for later. It was also considered all right for even first year student nurses to mix up a cocktail of soluble aspirin with antacid liquid, flavoured with red codeine cough linctus, in a little glass measuring cup, to give relief to someone experiencing post-operative wind-pains, or a headache. It was wonderful when this mixture worked, not just because it gave relief to the patient but because it meant that night sister wouldn't have to come back to the ward! They had to be sure to collect the glass measuring cups to wash before morning so there would be enough for the next pill-round—no little disposable plastic cups for them yet, but their manufacture was fast approaching.

Alice did have one scary moment in her second year, which

served as a salutary lesson to her to not to be too gung-ho with the night sedations. Alice had the sleeping tablets in their little bottles with her when she was giving out cups of drinks on one evening duty and she had been around the ward dispensing to everyone, and returned to collect the used cups. She started from left to right in the main-ward and arrived at an old lady's bed near the door and saw immediately, and to her horror, that the woman was unconscious with a dribble of dark-brown fluid coming out of the side of her mouth. Alice's first reaction was: Who should she call for help? Would resuscitation be needed? How could she explain this to the sister-in-charge? What would happen to Alice? She did as they had all been taught, and pulled the screens around her patient quickly, spoke to her clearly and called her by name, checked her pulse and, when there was no response although she had a pulse, she rubbed along her ribcage using her knuckles for painful stimuli to stir her. The little old lady opened her eyes in dismay and spat out the remainder of the chocolate bar she was eating when she had fallen asleep thanks to her sleeping pills that Alice had helped her take! Sometimes a fright like that is important to the learning experience, Alice thought later, but the feeling of being the cause of someone's possible overdose was a nasty one to remember, and she was forever cautious when giving out any medications. Years later she was to witness what she considered were over-cautious rules being introduced that saw many drugs, including sedatives, checked at the bed-side by two nurses after they had also been entered in a register. Times had indeed changed, but they also made nurses duties a bit more cumbersome and even more time consuming.

Study-block was a reprieve in many ways and an opportunity to be social too. Alice and her group were allowed to have a 'block party', a mixed gathering, in a room beneath the nurses' home and they could invite friends, even boyfriends if they had one, and serve beer, cordial and light refreshments. It was something to really look forward to, an occasion to dress up for in colourful mini-dresses and knee-high boots and the night had the added bonus of not needing to be arranged around shifts—their hours were nine a.m. till four p.m. while they were in 'block'.

Alice didn't have a boyfriend then. She always hoped that she would meet someone at the office where she had once worked, or on the Thursday nights when she went to hear groups play in the back streets of London where men and boys asked the most interesting girls, in their very short skirts with makeup and hair styles like Cleopatra, or hair like exaggerated beehives, to dance. But she was never asked to dance or go out by anyone. She did have a couple of dates that were set up for her by Jenny after their fruit-picking frolic, but they definitely were not her type of men, there was no future with them. She knew this, because they had no courtesy, no kindness, they were not interesting to talk to, and she hated the idea of kissing them. She was starting to think that it was time she found a boyfriend and as it turned out she soon did find one.

The first block party was organised by the most outgoing members of their group—and the guest list was by invitation only. Jharma took it upon herself to invite every young man she met in the hospital to come along. A patient on her new surgical ward, who was being treated for late-stage bowel cancer, had a good-looking son who was a regular visitor. Jharma met him on the stairs one day as she was going off duty and invited him to bring his friends and come to the party. He was working with his father on some works that were underway at the hospital and he thought that the invitation would be a nice distraction from his arduous tasks as a labourer. To put it frankly, it was clear that his intentions were licentious. Nurses were perceived to be a good bet for a fun night out in those days, and he was very keen for that.

A trestle table was laid with bottles of beer, cordials of orange and lemon, paper cups, and bowls of potato crisps and salted peanuts. The lights were turned down and festive paper streamers were strewn around the room in the basement. Alice was not at ease in this sort of environment, however inviting it looked. She took her time dressing and removed her rollers at the very last minute when she realised that she couldn't delay any longer. The others would wonder where she was, because she had disappeared as soon as the room was prepared. She flicked her fair hair up at the ends, combed it over her right eye and headed downstairs, once the evening was underway.

She always knew she was no beauty—classic beauty relied on symmetry of features she always thought—and she knew her features held no obvious attraction for the opposite sex, not like her friend Jenny who seemed to be attractive to everyone—but Alice still thought she was basically quite nice-looking, and she knew she had intelligent conversation and things to say once she overcame her inherent shyness. She had things to share with others—stories to tell too—and she was young if not nubile. Surely, she would appeal to someone, she thought. With this determination to show herself in a positive light, she helped herself to a paper cup of half beer and half cordial that night and tried to socialise within the group.

How she came to be sitting on Jack's knee discussing the need for twice daily cleaning of teeth and regular dental checks was beyond her memory after two cups of beer with the undiluted squash, but that is how the night ended up. And that was the precursor to a large part of her life. He was twenty and she was nineteen. They dated—and parted—married and had children together and parted. But that was all to come; in the meantime, for Alice, there was a career to be forged, knowledge to be accumulated, many lives to be lived, and half a world to be travelled in search of happiness and self-fulfilment. She also had stories to tell and a book to write.

CHAPTER FOUR
Learning and Growing…
Cleaning and Caring

Nurses were always involved in a hands-on occupation: they literally and physically learnt on the job, acquiring skills to help them identify sounds and smells and patient's responses to aid in diagnoses, while catering to the needs of everyone. Because the wards were filled by patients with complex and challenging conditions, many of which were only scantily recorded in the only text books that were available to them, student nurses would try to be at a bedside for a clinical instruction session lead by a senior doctor in a crisp white coat over his dark suit and tie leading his flock of trainee-doctors in similar attire. Student nurses were not asked to contribute or comment as a rule, and often the patients themselves weren't involved—everyone was just there to listen and observe—but a nurse's input was often useful to the session, providing information about fluid intake, urinalysis, wound healing, and preparations for discharge, which sister usually provided. The white coat was all powerful, and there was no doubt about who was in charge. Sometimes a student nurse was asked to help a patient lean forward or turn on their side, or there was a gesture from sister to tell her to clear the overbed table for the patient to lean on so that that chest sounds could more easily be heard with a stethoscope by the medical staff. There were often questions about the nature of the sputum that had been collected; was there blood present, was it viscous or fluid and how much had been emptied that day? Nurses knew these things; they collected and emptied the steel spittoons into the sluice in the pan room. This was not always an easy thing to do because the sticky secretions stuck tenaciously to the sides of the steel containers, and then to the sides of the porcelain sluice refusing to be flushed away and often leaving blood-stained streaks behind. This was a world of smokers and lung disease was prevalent.

There were many chores and activities which took place in the pan-room that tested the sensibilities and stomachs of the young nurses none of which could be shirked. There was no doubt that these chores were part of the '*job description*', though no such term was ever used. Testing urine for Ph, sugar, ketones and blood was not as simple as a multilayered chemical impregnated stick stuck into the voided urine in a bedpan or urinal then—instead there were little bottles of various tablets to drop into glass tubes which sometimes had to be boiled up with a Bunsen burner flame applied to the bottom of the tube and the contents checked for colour when the bubbling stopped. And sometimes the bubbles overflowed the tube just to add to the complexity of the procedure! Junior nurses also had the dubious honour of cleaning pans and other receptacles in a sink full of hot water using bristle brushes and scouring pads till they shone. Later automatic bed-pan washers became available but there was no satisfaction in that for an assiduous cleaner or student nurse/handmaidens like Alice, who took pride in their work. Stainless steel bedpans were very cold to the touch and conscientious nurses would warm a pan before placing it under a patient and cover it over with a cloth before removing it to the sluice after use. There were bed-pan warmers on each ward—a heated trolley where pans could be stacked and the trolley wheeled into the main ward at specific times in the day. Patients were encouraged to wait till pan-rounds for their toilet needs when two nurses could be available to assist if they were not able to use the over-bed hand-bar to lift themselves up for the pan to be slipped underneath them. Plastic bed pans, urinals, vomit bowls and kidney dishes, along with flimsy paper covers, came into general use a few years later, but for the young students at St Helens, in Alice's time, they were just a space-age concept. Plastic was indeed a welcome invention for many items like bed pans, making them lighter and easier to empty, but they never looked properly clean and hygienic like the old steel variety, Alice always thought. And anyway, an hour spent in the pan-room was an hour of solitude and reprieve from relentless ward-duties and away from the ever-critical eye of sister.

CHAPTER FIVE
Stress and More Stress

Alice became unwell during her first rotation on the medical ward. The sister-in-charge was so terrifying to her that she was too fearful to knock on her office door to even ask a question. One day, she thought, she must overcome this feeling if she was ever going to survive and become a *'real nurse'* and she bravely tapped on the glass of the partly open office door while sister was sitting behind her big wooden desk. Alice asked, *'May I come in and look at the chart of the new admission?'* and with a nod of her head, sister allowed her to come into the inner sanctum. With legs threatening to give way under her, Alice found the chart she wanted and read that the young patient was scheduled to have a *'biopsy'* that afternoon but not really understanding what a biopsy entailed, or what part of the body was involved, Alice turned to face the sister and asked her what it meant. She hadn't yet seen many procedures—she was only a few months into her training and was still learning the terminology that eventually became like a second language to her. Big mistake to ask a question on this occasion! If she wasn't already fearful in this place, the harsh reply from the sister to *'go and find out for yourself, nurse!'* compounded her anxiety. Alice would come to know about her anxiety and understand it as a stress-response, like the one that the night-sister induced in her in later months and something she would have to come-to-terms with and deal with, but from then on whenever she was in the presence of this particular ward-sister, or even saw her walking down the corridor, she would feel herself shaking, her heart thumping in her chest and her legs hardly able to keep her upright. It was only a matter of time before she became unwell in this environment and developed several boils, including one at the back of her nose and she had to be admitted as a patient for observation and antibiotic treatment.

The ten days Alice spent in St Helen's private ward was a god-send to her and she thought later that if this hadn't happened, she might well have considered leaving her training altogether—but she knew she wasn't going anywhere; and she had nowhere to go anyway. Her hospital stays not only took her off ward duties but gave her an opportunity to experience what it felt like to be a patient and observe how she was treated and how she was looked after. There were no junior nursing students working on this ward—it was a 'Private Ward' for sick staff and wealthy fee-paying people from both England and overseas, not NHS patients. Everyone had the very best of care and attention but it was still a working-ward—being a private patient didn't mean you wouldn't encounter the indignities of illness—and death was the same for everyone regardless of their station in life, she soon realised. There was a bonus on this ward too—patients were served 'real' coffee which was brewed up overnight with the addition of egg-shells to the pan (Alice never understood why; but the coffee tasted very good) and all food was individually prepared from a menu and a selection could be made the day before. She heard the sounds of the ward at night and although she was in a four-bed room and not a long ward like she had been working on before she became sick, the comings and goings were the same. Dimmed lights didn't take away the activities or make them difficult to hear or imagine, they just made them harder to observe.

The ward sister who she had been terrified of, dropped by with a little bunch of flowers for her. She didn't stay to chat, but her face was friendly and she smiled when she said, 'Get better soon!' Alice was relieved by this, but as it turned out she didn't go back to that ward again so she never had to test that 'friendliness'.

She had no visits from her family while she was an 'in-patient' and in fact she wondered later if she had even told them about her being ill, but they were getting ready for the big transition in their family life and they were very busy. Her father had taken early retirement from the forces, and with his *'golden-handshake'* sum in the bank, was preparing to emigrate to Australia. New Zealand had been an option, Alice learned, but they finally settled on Melbourne. Her mother approved of all the English sounding names of towns around the coast and along with a firm belief in the truth of all the advertising campaigns utilising sea, sand and surf to their best advantage that bombarded the television and street posters in England to attract migrants, they were happily prepared for the major transition in their lives. They had hoped to travel by sea—a pleasant way to get to Australia for Ten-Pound Poms back then—but a shipping strike delayed their departure for many weeks and they eventually took their less preferred option of an air-flight. For Alice this meant a final visit with them on a picnic on a south coast beach, and a lunch at the airport just before their departure with her uncle and aunt joining the group. She searched her memory to try to remember if her older brother and his wife had been there on this occasion but she could never recall and then when it became important for her to remember to include in her story, there was no one to ask about it. She just knew that she wasn't sad at her family going so far away, they had not been really close for some time, but contrarily and in the way of human nature, within a couple of months of them leaving Alice became depressed about what she came to think of as being 'abandoned' by them. She was often tearful at having no home to go to in her time off, and she missed her talks with her mother terribly, but she came to see that this was quite a selfish view for her to hold fast to and perhaps her feelings were accentuated by her recent illness and in fact she actually had much to be contented about. Many of her fellow students were very far away from their own homes and, in truth, South Africa, India, Ireland, Malaysia and Scotland were not places to visit on a weekend trip in those days. Later—much later—Alice was to smile at her recollection that people in the south of England would never think of taking a long-haul trip to the north of England in those days, when people in Australia would travel thousands of miles for a week's holiday. Eventually even post-war Britons came to learn that overseas travel was something within their reach—but not in the 1960s.

It took Alice a while to come to terms with her new circumstances and almost inevitably, she clung to anything or anyone who contributed to her sense of belonging, anyone who created a life contact for her and took away the feeling that she was left behind, alone and without support. Her friendship with Jack, the young man she had met at the block-party filled that void to some extent and she allowed their relationship to develop despite her misgivings. He was not always kind to her, and he was very immature—he understood nothing of the life she had had with her family nor anything of her travels nor of her work as a nurse. Not perfect, she knew, but he was good company, picked her up for dates and made her laugh often.

Her friendship with Monica was similar—not perfect, somewhat inequal in many ways and not unlike what she had with Jenny all those years ago, except that this time Alice actually had the more outgoing social role in their friendship despite her insecurities—and Monica was not seeking to expand her own social horizons in any way at all. Alice told stories that Monica liked to hear about her life that was so very different from Monica's own as a very much loved only-child of elderly parents living in the Midlands. At some level they connected as companions and were viewed as inseparable friends by their group. Alice suspected that Monica was too admiring of her at times, but they never discussed anything so personal although they talked about their work-lives a great deal. When Alice met Phillip, in the third year of their training and broke off her relationship with Jack, there was no doubt that Monica was quite pleased at the turn of events and wholeheartedly supported her in the decision. No story of a relationship break-up is ever as simple as that though, and there were some trying times and disappointments that Alice had with Jack that led her towards someone else. Jack was indiscreet in some of his liaisons, admitting that he cancelled dates with her to meet up with a married woman on at least one occasion, Alice was hurt but she reasoned that he was very young, younger than her by two years, and she had no right to expect that he would be faithful to her and yet she knew she wanted that. The pain of knowing that he did not respect her or her feelings was hurtful in itself and enough reason to stop seeing him, but knowing that she couldn't share with him the sadness and happiness that she saw in her everyday nursing life, or share with him the stories that she was beginning to collect in her head was all beginning to tell on her, and she knew she should stop right there, but she didn't—not then.

CHAPTER SIX
The Story of Sam

Days turned to nights, nights turned to days with weeks spent in the classroom learning and perfecting skills to put into practice on the wards—and inevitably, for all that knowledge to be applied to written and practical examinations which would lead to a state-recognised qualification in due time. Every day a new thing to experience, every patient a new life, with a story to consider and wonder about and to try to understand. The *'why'* of disease, the *'what'* of its manifestations and the *'how'* of its management was a huge part of Alice's mellowing adaptation to the world she was in. However, she was still often troubled by the life and death events that were part and parcel of her days.

Sam's story was one of many that she had come across but it touched her deeply and reinforced to her that she must not ever make hasty judgments of anyone or anything without careful consideration of all the facts.

Sam was admitted to the medical ward in the late afternoon of Alice's midweek split-shift when she was physically tired and she was looking forward to the end of it when she could just fall into bed. She had a day off the following day—and a day to recover seemed to be all she needed, but she was young then and tiredness didn't sit on her face and leave dark circles under her eyes as it did in later life.

It was Thursday; but one day was much like another to all the students—rosters were prepared weeks in advance and all they needed to do was check what the week and day was to know how their time would be spent. There was a weeks' holiday coming soon when she planned to go and visit her brother and his wife and baby for a few days, travelling by comfortable air-conditioned bus through charming villages and small market towns and allowing herself to doze, read and doze again in the way of all long-distance coach-travellers.

Her day had started at six a.m. and the afternoon break only allowed enough time for her to take a steamy bath, with a handful of fragrant crystals from Avon which dissolved slowly into the water—a thoughtful present from a fellow student for her recent birthday—in the old-fashioned and dimly-lit bathroom down the corridor from her room with its plentiful, soothing hot water.

Alice's family were already settled into their new home in Australia and her nursing training was moving on, her knowledge increasing, her skills developing and her thoughts maturing. But she was soon to have her belief system challenged, her lack of understanding about the world and the amazing resilience and goodness of people in the face of great sadness and uselessly insidious and carelessly acquired infection. She would also soon come to see how compassionate love looked and acted, and this was new to her and it touched her deeply.

Sam had tertiary syphilis, and was rapidly developing 'general paralysis of the insane', she heard at the handover of patients' from the morning to the evening staff, when she went back on duty. Later she read more about him in the doctors' notes in the office. Sam was young, fair haired and slim to the point of skeletal emaciation and he had a strange loping gait—seeming to step forward and then hesitating before bringing his foot down to the ground—which she had noted when she first saw him walking in the corridor and at the time it made Alice want to reach forward and help him at every step to stop him from falling. It was evening visiting time before she had a chance to look after him properly. He was in a single room along the main corridor and she knocked and opened the door to see a beautiful young woman sitting beside his bed. She had a little girl with curly blond hair sitting on her knee and a shy boy of about five years with black hair standing beside them. The boy looked just like his mother, which she clearly was, and Alice saw that the girl looked like Sam—but Sam as he might have been, not the skeleton of him that sat on the side of the bed, leaning forward, as if he was just about to get up and leave the room.

This was not the first time in the first eighteen months of her nursing career that Alice had to rearrange her thoughts, check her reaction to what she saw, or smelled, in case her eyes and the turn of her head gave her away. She was dismayed to realise that her preconception of Sam when she saw him in the corridor and after she knew his terminal diagnosis, was very judging—she had not pictured him with a beautiful family and a caring wife. Alice had read that he had travelled overseas in his work; and he was an educated man who had taught English at university in Ethiopia. She initially wrongly assumed that he must have availed himself of sex with prostitutes in his travels who had infected him with the disease which was now ravaging his body, and prematurely ending his life.

The truth was that Sam had been unmarried at the time of his sojourn in Africa, and fell in love with a young woman who worked with him. They had a necessarily very private relationship—mixed race relationships were criminal and punishable by law in many countries in those days. When he sailed back to his home in England, he knew that time in his life, and that relationship, was over and soon afterwards he met and married his beautiful Judith. She was an editor with a major publishing firm and she helped him put together the stories of his time in Ethiopia, and they settled into a loving, caring life with their young children.

He had ignored the early signs of his infection, the mild rash, the unsightly scabby chancres in his groin which healed spontaneously, and life went on normally until he started to develop fevers, lost some weight and some hair, and had vague rashes on his torso, but these symptoms also foxed him, and his wife, with their origins and so he had sought no treatment. This phase went into a dormant stage and he improved and they just got on with their lives. Their children were conceived without any difficulty within five years after they had married. By some freak chance Judith did not contract the disease and so nor did their babies who might have gone on to develop congenital syphilis.

By the time Sam presented at St Helen's outpatients department for investigation of the neurological signs he was developing (not just his hesitant gait and poor coordination, but also slurred speech and memory loss), it was too late for treatment—he was rapidly entering into the paralytic stage of the disease and his lifetime was limited.

If only, if only, he had been diagnosed earlier and been treated. Penicillin was available in the 1960s and arsenic-based medications had been successful in the past, but sitting patiently on the wooden bench with his wife, outside the doctor's room in outpatients, waiting for his name to called, Sam wouldn't have known what the end of his days looked like.

Sexually transmitted disease was not new in the world, Alice had learned from her reading: syphilis was widely thought of as the oldest and most lethal because of its devious nature—tricking the sufferer into a false sense of complacency after the initial symptoms—and history was rife with examples of famous figures who had, or were thought to have had, the disease. Picasso, Al Capone—who was reported to be certifiably insane due to late-stage syphilis at the time of his death—and Hitler, although never confirmed, was thought to have been on his way to general paresis due to his evident *'delusions of grande*ur'. Oscar Wilde, Toulouse Lautrec and even Karen Blixen, one of Alice's favourite authors who had contracted the bacterium from her husband and was given arsenic treatment which made her infertile, were also cited as sufferers.

There were cartoon-signs posted on the back of public-toilet doors that Alice and her fellow nurses noted and laughed about, which announced that it was *'no use standing on the seat, the spirochaete can jump three feet!'*. There was health information everywhere in her life, Alice came to realise; in public toilets, in magazines, some of it amusing, some unbelievable, but in the 1960s it was not explicit, it was euphemistic, only hinting that infection could be caught by anyone, anywhere. She reflected years later, that it wasn't until the AIDS epidemic of the 1980s through extensive marketing and prevention campaigns on television and in the press, that the general public was chillingly left in no doubt about its spread and origins.

The love and caring that Alice witnessed between Judith and Sam and their children in the week before he was transferred to the nearby mental health facility (still called an insane-asylum in those days and where Alice would have a fortnight's training visit in the near future), was heartbreaking to witness. She learned all she could about syphilis; pouring through all the medical and nursing books she could find and even without the benefit of computer-generated knowledge, she learnt a great deal. She researched how it was transmitted, how Sam's next stage would happen and how it could have been prevented. And she thought to herself that she hoped she would never witness this spirochaete's destructive power again.

As it turned out, Alice did see it again. Fifty years later in a Vietnamese clinic in Melbourne where she administered vaccinations and treatments on her days off, there was a young woman patient, who spoke very little English, with a second stage syphilitic infection. She had recently arrived in Australia from Hanoi where she had worked in the sex industry and she came to the clinic for her weekly penicillin doses in the hope that her condition could be treated in time. As Alice drew the thick white antibiotic solution up into the syringe and prepared to administer the injection, she had the opportunity to observe her patient's poor physical state, her pock-marked skin, the thinness of her arms and legs and without much common language to take the place of any real communication, after giving the injection, she placed the empty syringe in the tray and put her arms around the young woman. The encounter lasted just seconds but the smiles they had for each other before she left said it all. Alice wished that she had been able to show Sam and Judith the compassion she felt for them all those years before, but displays of affection were not encouraged in her nursing training and anyway she wouldn't have had the daring to display her emotions so openly in those days.

CHAPTER SEVEN
The Story of Grace

How quickly night-duty stints came around, Alice thought as she busied herself tidying up her little room. It felt to her a bit like 'spring cleaning'—and sometimes she needed a reason to do something to give her impetus and a purpose and the impending two weeks of night duty was enough of a trigger on this occasion. Her room cleaning had been on her mind but she had not had the energy for it, she felt caught in a vortex of work, work and more work—each day melding into the next without any clear definition between them and without any goals being set and met. She would really go to visit her brother and his wife and new baby when she had time off again, she promised herself once again. She had not been well enough to go when she had first planned, and then her second planned visit had to be delayed because of roster changes, but this next time she would definitely go—but first she had to go through another round of living in the 'nether-world' where sensible people went to bed at a sensible time in the dark and woke refreshed as daylight came. She didn't know then about the effects of melatonin in regulating sleep and neither did she think that there was any harm in taking one or two of those little coloured pills that she handed out to patients willy-nilly and unaccounted for, if they would help her get a few hours' sleep before she went on duty, which was all she perpetually craved. But go back on night duty she did; slept or not, prepared or not, for what might present itself.

'Be prepared', had been instilled in all of them; hours spent preparing rooms as an example of an incoming patient's needs, laying trolleys with equipment that just might be required according to lists and guidelines printed on foolscap sheets which were stored in a folder in the ward office. 'Possible pneumothorax', an instruction over the 'phone from the casualty department ('casualty' was a euphemistic term for everything to do with health and sickness, it seemed to Alice), or: 'hip fracture—traction with weights (advise night porter to bring frame and weights to the ward). And a very bad call to receive at two a.m. 'Incoming road-accident—prepare for admission of two people with multiple injuries possibly within one hour.'

But the worst message of all worst messages, received on the first night of her rotation onto the gynaecological (gynae) ward was: 'emergency admission—young female with fever and vaginal bleeding. Prepare a bed in the ward.'. It was early in the shift when the call came, the main ceiling lights had already been turned off for the night, and the single lamp on an angled stand on the central table in the ward was on, some of the beds were still lit by bedside lamps directed onto books being read in the reduced light of the ward—there were no overhead television screens giving-off flickering light then, that was still a few years away. A small-screen television was available for ambulant patients in the ward sitting-room and then only at strictly specified times. This night, as on most nights, the wards were quiet; respectfully so, with just the occasional sound of matches striking a light for a last cigarette.

Dutifully, Alice with her fellow student, who was six months ahead of her in her training and leading the preparations, drew the screen-curtains around an empty bed in the long ward, turned back the covers neatly and placed a rubber sheet underneath the coarse linen draw-sheet to protect the flock-filled mattress from potential soiling. Together they collected and arranged; rectangular cotton absorbent pads (cut from a long roll into batches of five and prepared by nurses with a few spare minutes on their shift when they also rolled freshly washed bandages ready for use), a patient's gown (opening at the back), a spare draw-sheet, neatly folded, a glass thermometer standing in pink disinfectant in a bracket attached to the wall, and a sphygmomanometer to check the blood pressure, and together with all the relevant charts, they laid them out neatly on the high bed table. They brought a metal stand to the bedside ready for an infusion bottle and stepped back to check that they had covered all eventualities. *'Textbook set-up'*, they whispered proudly to each other, and went to check on the patients in the side wards while they waited for their admission.

What they weren't expecting to see on the trolley that was pushed in by the night porter, guided briskly by the night-sister in a white gown over her uniform, was a patient as young as they both were, with long dark hair and pale fair skin (Irish possibly, Alice thought vaguely). The patient's light, slim body was limp and they had to help transfer her onto the bed using long metal poles that slotted into either side of the canvas sheet spread underneath her on the trolley. They had already removed the head of the before she arrived. She felt hot to the touch as Alice and her colleague, under sister instructions, moved her gently from one side to the other to remove the canvas and allow the night porter to return to the casualty department with his trolley for his next duties and instructions. The patient had a strange body odour, Alice noted, not that of a menstrual flow—all women knew what that smelt like in the days of sanitary pads and belts, before internal tampons were freely available and well used—no, the blood on her pads smelt of fish somehow, and it was tinged with green and there was a lot of it. They changed her pads again and again, and wrapped them up carefully in a square green cloth for later inspection in the sluice; they wore no gloves but did put on nurses' gowns to protect their aprons. Her temperature was high— *'Pyrexia. 101 point 4'*, Alice told sister when she enquired—but her face and hands were cold and the skin on her legs had patches of blue on them, not blue veins but mottled skin tinged with pink, nothing like Alice had seen before in her limited experience. The hospital night sister stayed at the bedside with her patient, taking over the space around the bed and making the patient her own. She calmly reassured her, called her by name. '*Grace?*' she asked quietly, leaning into her ear and not wanting to disturb the other patients in the ward. *'Do you have any pain?'* Grace moved her head, indicating 'no'. *'Doctor is on his way,'* sister said gently. Alice stored away for future reference how to speak to someone so young and obviously so sick, and waited near the bedside for instructions on what she might be needed to do to help, watching carefully for signs from sister as she coordinated proceedings. When the doctor arrived with his white coat unbuttoned and swinging behind him in his hurry, sister asked Alice and her fellow student to go and attend to a patient's call bell that could be heard buzzing on the wall outside the swing doors of the ward, and then she instructed them to take a forty-five-minute supper break off the ward as was usual practice about this time. It was after midnight and routines had to be kept to so the staff-nurse on duty came to take their place. Later Alice understood that night sister had also thought that this was not an occasion to be used for clinical teaching of junior nurses.

  The light above Bed 10, Grace's bed, was still on, Alice saw through the door when she got back, but the curtains were not pulled around the bed anymore—four curtained screens on castor-wheels were in place and shielding the view of Grace's bed from the other patients—and from Alice's view at first. But then Alice saw the steel resuscitation trolley standing beside the bed with a monitor and metal instruments on top and drawers open to expose rubber tubes and glass phials of medication and syringes. There was no other evidence of frantic efforts having taken place, no signs of the dramatic hurry to save a life, with pillows and bedhead removed and bright lights shining, as Alice was to witness many times in her future life as a nurse. A firm board, half as long as Grace was tall, had been placed underneath the draw-sheet—they could see where it overlapped the bed. There was no movement from the body on top of it; no hint that Grace was alive. Her body, up to her neck was covered with a clean sheet, tucked around her—her unnaturally pallid face in quiet repose with eyes shut like she was sleeping, was uncovered. There was clearly no hope that she could have been saved to live her life more fully and in a better time. There was quiet in the ward; and in the dim light Alice could see the expression of resignation on sister's face and on the faces of the doctors who had come to assist in the minutes after the emergency had been called. They were working around each other briskly and efficiently without words—charts being completed, glass intravenous bottles and tubes and phials with the tops snapped off—the detritus of a failed attempt to save a life—all being collected in large brown paper bags for later removal to the hospital basement for incineration. Grace's body would also soon be transported by a night porter to the basement, on a steel trolley and accompanied by a nurse (not Alice on this occasion), down in the stairwell lift and along the dimly lit corridors underneath the hospital where the green-gowned and masked staff on duty were waiting at the mortuary door.

Grace had died from septicaemia, the medical report showed—a raging bacterial infection taking over her organs faster than any available treatment could halt. She had arrived in England from the south of Ireland, from County Cork, to be an *au pair* to a London family just six months before. She was employed to care for their children, to cook and clean and be a part of their lives before she took up training at a prestigious school for nannies the following year when she turned eighteen.

'Back-yard abortions' were not uncommon in the years before the contraceptive pill was freely available for sexually active young women, though it was often prescribed in the guise of: *'to regulate menstruation'*. The stigma of illegitimate birth, especially following a teenage pregnancy, was emotionally charged then and judged as morally wrong, just as an abortion was judged as a deplorable waste of life, by the Church. Alice had seen the film *Alfie* which poignantly told the story of a mature, married woman who could not go ahead with an unwelcome pregnancy, and she had read books about the psychological and physical trauma suffered by those who became pregnant 'out of wedlock' and who (at significant cost), had sought out unscrupulous people, often poorly trained nurses and ill-equipped doctors, to abort their foetuses. But this was real this time, not just a story, not just a fiction; Grace was real, she had been flesh and blood and she died because of some lonely, botched, rough attempt to cause her to miscarry in the early weeks of her pregnancy. The sadness of what she had seen that night stayed in Alice's memory for the rest of her life.

CHAPTER EIGHT
Sharing the Load

So many things were happening so rapidly, so many experiences to unravel and understand and Alice and her cohorts looked forward to being in study block to share their tales with their tutor. Miss Bronsen used these opportunities to the hilt, encouraging discussion and using diagrams on charts and her coloured chalks on a blackboard to illustrate the anatomy and physiology of health and illness. But she didn't delve into their stories, or help them 'work through' issues that troubled them. With hindsight Alice saw that she was not emotionally engaged with her students which was her only downfall as their guide and teacher. There was no post-trauma counselling offered, no psychological de-briefing, but they had each other to talk with. And talk they did—followed by very long card games of Canasta or 500 in someone's room, accompanied by Cinzano and lemonade and puffing on menthol cigarettes, until the home sister rapped on the door and told them to get to bed.

Psychiatry and psychology had been around for many long years; Freud was mentioned in some of the texts Alice read, and Librium (later Valium) was available and prescribed for anxiety and depressive states, but psychiatry still seemed to be regarded as a very secondary aspect of health as far as Alice could see. She had witnessed her father's melancholia many times in her growing up which had contributed to the distancing in their relationship, along with his abuse of alcohol, but it never occurred to her then that perhaps it has treatable if he had received the right help, and in later years she made him an apology for her lack of insight. Many people she knew still talked of psychology as *'mumbo-jumbo'*. 'Just get over it', and 'all things will pass' were commonly used phrases. This was still an era of the 'stiff upper lip' despite it being two decades past the end of the Second World War when freedoms were expanding exponentially.

Dressing freely, women were beginning to wear jeans like men, although it still raised eyebrows in the street; skirts were worn with hemlines above the knee and young people danced as individuals in time with a loud beat without words or touching. However, divorce, single-parenting and even sex before marriage were not acknowledged as a fact of life, and unmarried couples didn't move-in together. Oddly enough, Alice often thought, it had once been unusual to see people in the streets walking while eating, but not then, and it was considered perfectly acceptable to be sitting on a bench eating fish and chips from grease-proof paper wrapped in a piece of ordinary broadsheet newspaper. For those born in the post-war period, this new time, this new ideology with new freedoms was not easy to adjust to, and judgements were made that would not have been acceptable in this decade when Alice was remembering her past. Political correctness was an unknown, but etiquette was still the expected norm. Manners were important.

On their third study block the curriculum included a rare lecture to be given by someone other than Miss Bronsen. They listened with credulous admiration to a young doctor, not in a white coat but sporting a tweed jacket with leather elbow patches and a green knitted woollen tie, who sat on a stool at the front of the class and introduced them to the wonders of the mind. He spoke about the effects of drugs on mood and behaviour, and the future of brain surgeries such as lobotomy, and about Electro Convulsive Therapy (ECT) and so many other things. They heard that homosexuality was still considered a mental aberration in manuals on Mental Disorders. Alice had no knowledge of same-sex relationships, and although they were sometimes hinted at when she was in the Middle East and she noticed Arab men holding hands, she had never seen men kiss men or women kiss women in any way but affectionately on the cheek. She knew she had so much to learn and understand about life still.

The lecture by this young psychiatrist was perfectly timed because the group was soon to start a two-week stint at the local mental hospital. The terms 'mental hospital' and 'insane asylum' had been dropped from signposts and maps some years before, but amongst themselves the students still used the terminology, and they were all in some trepidation about what they might witness during their visits.

They went in pairs to this hospital, and Alice went with Monica, travelling to and fro by bus in their uniforms and capes, which they had been given special permission to do. They were greeted on arrival at the door of the impressively beautiful brick building by the matron, who was tall and slim in a dark blue dress which accentuated her slimness and she wore a white belt and a white frilled cap pinned to her greying hair. She had a pleasant smile for them which was not altogether spoiled by her nicotine-stained teeth. She ushered them in the door of the main building at the end of a gravel drive which they had walked down from the bus-stop after being let through the high gates in the ivy-covered brick wall surrounding the grounds by a guard.

On reflection later, Alice and Monica thought the matron's manner might have said: 'Quick, come in before anyone gets out!' Paranoia wasn't something they knew much about at the time, but they were clearly overthinking and had distinct feelings of apprehension about what they were going to see and experience. This visit consolidated their friendship in those years as they laughed about so many things together and off-loaded many of their concerns about what they had witnessed.

The tour of the facility started on the ground floor with brief glimpses of the rooms off a spacious entry with its high ceilings and colourful tessellated tiles on the floor. All doors had shiny metal signs attached by small screws on the top and bottom declaring in turn—*Matron's Office, (knock before entering), Bursar; Almoner* (by appointment only); *Psychiatric Clinic; Pharmacy,* and so on. The term 'Social Worker' was becoming more commonly used in Alice's nursing days, but the ancient term '*Almoner'* persisted in theory, and on door signs, although the giving of money or food to the poor was not really in the job-description anymore. Alms (the dispensing of money to the disadvantaged) was now a State responsibility through welfare programs—the National Health Service (NHS) having come into being just after Alice was born. But matrons still ran hospitals in Alice's training days answering to the board but with all the power to conduct hospital business that a CEO has in more recent times. Alice often thought, in her maturity, that it was once a much more efficient way to do it all—no separation of powers to get in the way of good business!

The old timber stairs creaked under their footsteps as they were led up to the second floor by the matron. They were guided by the highly polished banister while they negotiated the deep time-worn treads which immediately brought to Alice's mind Thornfield Hall in Charlotte Bronte's *Jane Eyre*—she must remember to say this to Monica, she thought. *Twenty, twenty-*

one, twenty-two, Alice counted to herself at each stair with plenty of time to wonder why there was no carpet to soften the stairway. They shared an occasional sidelong glance with wide-eyes of mutual questioning. Alice and Monica had few expectations for this visit, little significant prior knowledge of mental illness and its manifestations and treatments other than the charming lecture given by the good-looking psychiatrist with the green woollen tie—and they were totally unprepared for what they were to see and experience.

The first door that Matron opened with her *'set of many keys'*, was into a room furnished with leather winged-armchairs facing each other in groups of four, with small, round wooden tables on pedestals in between them. There was no one in the room—*and just as well,* Alice thought. The air had a chill to it, there was no heating although there was a large fireplace surrounded by an exquisitely carved mantelpiece with corbels of acorns embedded in it. They had time to take in the whole look and feel of this space as the matron explained that the room was used for group counselling sessions that were held weekly for those inmates who could benefit from this 'new innovation'. Alice, with her early eye for such things as decor, thought that the introduction of some fresh flowers and a few chair cushions would have all the room needed to make it more friendly and welcoming for any 'inmates' wanting to bare their souls. But she was in no position to comment on this, and anyway there was no time. They were soon moved on to the end of the corridor where another door opened to Matron's keys but this time there was a second door, a bar-grilled door with a heavy lock which was not opened to them. Through the bars they could see about twenty women, some in groups around a table with playing cards in their hands rocking slowly backwards and forwards, not speaking, not looking at each other, not interacting or responding to the matron and her visitors behind the grille. Some were pacing around the room, stopping to occasionally call out, to swear at no-one or anything in particular. They were all dressed in pale green tunics, some were barefoot, some had worn-tartan slippers on their feet, some were bedraggled, looking unwashed, but they all looked as if they belonged together. They were a homogenous group. *'They're waiting for their next medications and some are going to be picked up for treatments soon,'* Matron told them matter-of-factly. 'It will soon *be morning tea-time and they get to join the men in the dining room, which is a nice social activity in their day.'*

Matron completed the tour by briskly escorting them into a series of small wards with cots on either side where there were several babies and small children many with severe limb deformities and obvious mental abnormalities. In a number of cots there were infants with varying degrees of hydrocephalus, being attended to by nurses in green gowns tied at the waist; some were pouring milky liquid into in-situ nasal feeding-tubes. There was no delay here, no pausing in these wards. In some of the rooms, babies and young children, some crying with cat-like sounds, some just lying quietly prone in their cots, heads and necks extended with blank eyes, were being tended; some being bathed and having nappies changed by the nurses moving efficiently from one to another of their charges. The matron greeted the nurses cheerily and asked if there were any problems. She was so friendly to everyone that Alice began to wonder if she had a totally wrong impression of 'matrons.

Matron didn't delay here long enough for Alice and Monica's questions, just enough time for them to take in the scene, the smells, the sadness in those rooms even without knowing the circumstances of their births or their family histories. But they also noticed the care that was being taken as limbs were moved and heads cradled—and there was a strong sense of kindness here and an all-encompassing smell of Johnsons baby powder that they remembered later.

They were not to visit these rooms, this area, again during their time there, but they talked about the day and what they had seen, on the trip home, upstairs on the double-decker bus, back to St Helens, and for a long time afterwards. They no longer referred to it as a mental asylum—it became the '*sad hospital*' to them.

As students-in-training visiting this institution they were here to learn what was on their curriculum to learn; and they were also soon to learn a great deal about psychotropic medications and treatments and their effects and administration. It wasn't all medications and treatments—there were activities that they saw some of the adult-inmates taking part in. Small groups were gardening in the beautiful, expansive grounds where Alice and Monica shared the packed-lunch they had brought with them kindly prepared by the kitchen staff and left on the bench for them to pick up in named brown paper bags. There were inmates painting with watercolours in a quiet room on the third floor and others playing soccer against teams from the local area, and always they were heavily supervised and observed by white-coated male-staff and uniformed nurses with bunches of keys attached to their belts.

Of all the experiences that Alice had in the first couple of years of her training, these two weeks in the psychiatric hospital (*the sad hospital*), surpassed even the time of intense clinical training in an eye hospital in the district local where they were assigned their own rooms for the duration of their stay, during their second year. Watching delicate eye surgery was a mandatory part of their training and had to be signed off as being attended in their little notebooks full of procedures for them to witness or complete. Standing in the operating theatre one day, gowned and masked, watching an eye being removed, Alice fainted for just the second time in her life! She knew that these memories would be imprinted and would last her whole lifetime—and of course they did, and eye-care became her least liked duty forever.

Times did change, technology did advance, but the mental illnesses of the men and women that they witnessed there at the *sad hospital* changed very little over the years. They did not simply get better and go home. The living conditions in hospitals like this were improved for a while and there was more freedom for the inmates who were stabilised on anti-psychotic medication or ECT therapy, but then places like this were closed in the 1980s and their care became a community issue, a community problem, a community conundrum, which seemed to Alice to have no possible chance of being alleviated in her lifetime. And as she wrote down her stories many years later, she reflected on the sadness of seeing ECT performed during this visit and later seeing all those lively minds full of clear and interesting memories like hers, dulled by repeated 'treatments.'

CHAPTER NINE
Reflections on Living

Alice had come to writing late in her life. Not that she hadn't dabbled in the pleasure of writing short stories, and long letters, on occasions, and she had always been an avid reader, but she had not written about herself before she started her memoir and she found that the impact of recalling and recording so much that was in her mind weighed heavily on her at times. She wrote about how she tried to describe to Monica the intensity of her feelings when she had to escort a young woman lying on a narrow steel trolley into a small room where an anaesthetist stood waiting to administer ECT. Monica was less emotional than Alice—took most things in her stride—her personality was less passionate, less insightful and less sensitive, but she still listened to Alice's description with interest. Monica had not had to witness any treatments—she was waiting in the ward to receive the patients back. Alice didn't have all the words to use then to describe what she saw, but her feelings were so strong that it would have been impossible for Monica not to have been stirred by what she said.

There was a trolley covered in a green cloth in the room, Alice told her, like a table set for afternoon tea, but with a voltage machine with graduated dials, a sort of radio, a padded mouth gag and various steel instruments on the top. There was one other nurse in attendance with Alice, and an anaesthetist holding a board with a piece of paper attached. After asking the patient her name, he made a note on the sheet with his fountain pen and handed it to her to sign with a pencil. He checked her hands to make sure she had no rings on her fingers but made no attempt to engage with her—her name was Ruth, Alice heard her say—nor did he explain the upcoming procedure. Alice knew from experience that doctors in more modern times were taught to give thorough explanations about everything. In fact, Alice often thought that sometimes, by 'reassuring' they often scared the living daylights out of their patients with too much information and detail, but in the ECT treatment that Alice was to witness this day, there was no prior explanation for Ruth who lay on her back with one pillow under her head and her long dark hair pulled back and covered with a white paper cap. Her brown eyes were vacant and un-engaged. Alice stood at the end of the trolley, as instructed, to keep out of the way, and watched as small electrode wires were attached to each side of Ruth's forehead, on her temples, and electric current was passed through her brain inducing involuntary convulsions Alice knew that the treatment was intended to relieve severe symptoms of some mental health conditions but she felt devastated by what she had witnessed, and had tears in her eyes as she helped the porter wheel Ruth's trolley back to the ward where Monica was waiting beside a freshly made up bed.

Later in the quiet of her room back at St Helens, Alice read everything she could find on ECT in books that she had brought back from the *sad hospital's* library and in the volume of medical history that she found in the nurses' library on the ground floor of the nurses' home. She read about the history of electro convulsive therapy, its effect, side-effects, manifestations in later life and the beneficial effects on the life of its recipients, and about procedural details; but she found nothing then of first hand experiences of the patients, telling of the devastation of losing the ability to manage one's own emotional response, of losing memory; only decades later were scholarly articles available to illuminate all that, and yet even then they still reassured that ECT was a valuable means of treating severe depression.

Alice had reason to remember Ruth and her treatment vividly. She met her again in the gynae ward at St Helen's when Alice was in her second year of training. She knew the time and details of this re-encounter by remembering the sunlight streaming through the windows of the four-bedded ward, which placed the time as early summer—the English sun was mild outside, but strong when reflected through the panes of the closed window and she had to pull the blind down beside Ruth's bed so she wouldn't be too hot.

At this stage in her training Alice was competent in managing intravenous infusions in their glass bottles but, without the benefit of electronic-pumps to regulate the flow of fluid, she had to count the drops going through the chamber using her fob-watch. Alice recognised Ruth from her *sad hospital* experience immediately when she came on duty and was doing her patient round, but Ruth didn't know her—her eyes were as blank as they were the first time, she had met her. Ruth was still under the effect of the anaesthetic and had been brought back from theatre by the porter and the theatre nurse whose shoes were covered in fabric boot-covers. Patients were handed over to the staff-nurse in charge who then instructed her students about what care would be needed—standard practice then and for many years that followed.

Ruth had just had a D and C (a dilatation and curettage) to rupture the foetal sac about twelve or fourteen weeks into her pregnancy; *'father unknown'* was recorded in her history. The other three beds in the room were also for D and C patients and all had as their addresses the mental institution where Ruth was a long-term resident and where Alice had first seen her. All of these women, some in their forties, were noted as being in the *'early stages of pregnancy'*. After theatre they were returned to the ward where infusions of Pitocin would induce contractions and speed up the whole unhappy process for them.

In the days before unionisation of nursing, there was no limit to the number of patients a nurse would look after on any one shift; and call bells were answered and requests dealt with by any nurse within earshot. On this particular afternoon Alice had the added responsibility of looking after all four of the IV infusions in the ward that Ruth was in when she came back from theatre, as well as two infusions in the main ward. Tasks were her responsibility that day, rather than specific patients. To say she was busy would have been an understatement at every level, but then things got worse for Alice. Returning from the store room with an armful of linen to change the draw-sheets under the theatre patients—there were no handy plastic-backed paper pads to use then—she watched in horror as she saw Ruth coming out of her room clutching her lower abdomen with blood trickling down her legs onto the floor, and the IV tubing hanging free from her arm. Alice dropped her bundle of linen and ran towards Ruth shouting for help, but before Alice could reach her, Ruth had expelled her small foetus and it hung from its cord between her legs. Alice had no training in this kind of emergency; so which issue should she address first… potential haemorrhage from the uterus, or foetal trauma, or even how to get her confused patient back to the safety of a bed… or should she lay her down on the floor? The ward sister arrived with a steel kidney-dish in her hands containing a pair of suture-scissors and two metal clamps and a green hand-towel covering the contents. She helped Alice get Ruth onto the bed before clamping the cord, laying the little pink aborted foetus, with its expelled placenta, in the steel dish and then she instructed Alice to take it to the pan-room and alert the other ward-staff to come and help.

The foetus was still alive, struggling to breathe, its tiny body no more than a few inches long but distinguishable as a human baby and this shocked Alice; she had not expected to see anything so well formed and later wondered what gestation Ruth actually was. Before the days of pregnancy ultrasounds early estimations were often inaccurate and made on physical examination and the mother's history, if she was able, or willing, to give it.

Although Alice had enough knowledge to know that these feeble efforts to breathe were not compatible with life and any effort by her to prolong its life would not be the right thing to do, she still found it excruciatingly painful to watch as it gave up its fight. In the 1960s babies weighing less than one kilogram (approximately twenty-seven or twenty-eight-weeks' gestation) were considered non-viable because there was not the apparatus to keep them alive. Because humidicribs, reliable mechanical ventilators or neonatal intensive care were not available at the time, most infants born more than three months premature would not survive. But things were changing, technology was advancing rapidly and within a decade the age of viability went from twenty-eight weeks to twenty-four weeks and Alice had the opportunity to deliver and care for many premature babies in her midwifery practice.

With some effort, Alice dried her tears, covered the foetus in the dish with the cloth, and returned to help clean up the mess in the corridor that Ruth had caused. She watched the remaining three patients in that ward like a hawk until they had all delivered their foetuses, with sister's help, then Alice washed and dressed the women in their clothes and they were collected by porters from their institution and returned to their locked-wards at the *sad hospital*.

How, Alice wondered often, had the opportunity to become pregnant presented itself to these women in their '*locked-wards*' and who had taken advantage of their mental incapacity so indecently? Male staff members were sometimes implicated and, when Alice and her cohorts gossiped together, they thought this too. But there was no knowing for sure, and this was a time before oral contraception (the Pill) was commonly available. There was a time coming when involuntary sterilisation of women with mental conditions by tubal ligation was discussed at length and became very controversial, but it was argued to be barbaric and against human rights by some. However, to Alice, having witnessed Ruth's ECT treatment and her *involuntary termination* (*physician approved*), she always harboured the thought that permanent prevention of pregnancy would have been a much better option for her.

Ruth may not have recognised her or acknowledged her, her eyes as vacant as when she first met her at her ECT treatment, but the memory of Ruth stayed with Alice. She was another of her patients who would never be forgotten.

CHAPTER TEN
A Singular Life

In her seventies and living alone, Alice knew she was becoming more reclusive as time passed. It was not intentional; her life just seemed to progress that way; she had travelled on her own a great deal after Kelly died. She had met many people, she had seen many places she wanted to write about, written her stories and talked about them in every place she could and to all manner of audience. In a way it seemed to her that she had no more need to go anywhere, no need to spend time with people from a sense of duty or of obligation and she didn't expect that anyone should spend time with her out of obligation either. She quite contentedly preferred to spend her time writing peacefully in her home while her memories were still vivid and still coming—and in fact refusing to go away. She also read anything and everything that was available to her, relying more on her laptop computer and her *Kindle* device than ever before. Buying books became less attractive to Alice after she had culled the shelves that Kelly had left filled to the hilt. She found giving them away quite distressing and almost disloyal to Kelly, and it took her a long time to do.

Although her reclusive lifestyle suited her, that is not to say she wouldn't have liked a little more help around the house from time to time—Edna came once a week to clean the floors and change the bed linen, but apart from taking out her kitchen rubbish to the large plastic garbage-bins at the front of her house for collection later in the week, there was little else she needed to do now that Alice lived basically in one living room, one bedroom and a kitchen. But the gathering dust on the mantelpiece and encroaching weeds in the garden were hard for her to ignore, and the fridge needed to be cleared out, she was well aware—but there was so much more she had to write still, so she would worry about those mundane trifles later.

While she pondered on her own reclusive existence, there came to her mind the memory of an elderly man who was admitted to the medical ward at St Helens where Alice was working in her third rotation. She thought of him as 'elderly', when in fact he would have been no older than she was now, but he was derelict, homeless, a pauper—which Alice certainly was not.

He was unkempt; his hair was long, grey, stringy and dirty under his oily flat-cap, his skin was marked with scabs and streaked with scratch marks between his fingers, in the crook of his arms, and, as she found out later, in the folds of his groins as well as between his buttocks and behind his knees: clear evidence of a scabies infestation. He was thin, undernourished, waif-like but his apologetic smile and clear blue eyes made Alice warm to him immediately. His name was Tom. His toe nails were so long that they curled around under themselves like antlers, and he smelled strongly of his dirt and lack of care. He smelled rancid, in fact, and on his right shin he had an ulcer (he told her that was what it was), with a dirty crepe bandage loosely wrapped around it. When Alice removed the bandage to clean beneath it, to her horror, she discovered maggots feeding on his skin. The ulcer wound was clean and healing and when Alice researched later, she learned that there were benefits in using maggots to clean wounds, and historically their use had been a common treatment, but her first reaction to this sight made her turn away so Tom wouldn't see her revulsion and rising physical nausea.

Tom was a challenge! Alice loved a challenge as all her fellow nurses also loved a challenge—something to undertake wholeheartedly and then to see the end results of their efforts—and, hopefully, make a difference in a life and in a community also, Alice reflected, as she and many of her group had done when they went forward into their careers as registered nurses.

After a cursory visit by the ward doctor, Tom allowed her—welcomed her in fact—to undertake his care. She bathed him in disinfectant diluted in a sitz-bath—an old-fashioned term Alice didn't come across again until many years later when she cared for women after childbirth who had perineal sutures following an episiotomy, and a sitz-bath was recommended as soothing and healing for them. For Tom, though she did a lot more—she washed his hair, used heavy-duty clippers on his nails, used antiparasitic lotion on his scabies sites, dressed him in hospital pyjamas and left him to rest in the clean sheets of his hospital bed, with a hot cup of sweet tea on his over-bed table.

As Alice worked on Tom's bodily treatments and care, preparing him for the tests he would soon undertake—all the blood tests and x-rays that the doctors had ordered (there were no scans or magnetic imaging available in those days, otherwise he would have been ordered them too; and all paid for by the NHS), she talked with him about his life. His Scottish family had cast him off him some years before, claiming that his lifestyle was bringing disgrace upon them, and his two adult sons no longer had any contact with him. He had been an accountant. There had been some dispute over money and property with his business partner, and Tom was made bankrupt. His wife died shortly after this family 'disgrace', when the boys were teenagers. The grief he felt at the loss of his wife put him into deep depression and he became increasingly withdrawn and unavailable to his children who were taken to live with their aunt—his wife's sister. Tom was soon homeless and surviving on the streets with his daily bottle of sherry wrapped discreetly in a brown paper bag. And he would have continued to live his life that way until inevitably he would be found one morning '*dead in the gutter*', as Tom told her—but fate intervened; instead, he collapsed in the off-license liquor shop in the High Street one Saturday morning and was brought into St Helens by a kindly ambulance crew.

When the results of his tests came through, the team of ward doctors in their habitual white coats over dark suits and collegiate striped-ties, gathered one morning around Tom's bed behind the screens drawn around them. The doctors checked his charts, inspected his legs, talked to each other about the results and the findings that the junior residents reported on, and then the senior physician told Tom from the end of the bed: '*Sorry, old fellow, the results aren't good. Looks like you have a cancer in your liver which has spread to your lungs and bones. Nothing to be done; we'll just keep you comfortable. Do you have any questions? I am sure that the girls here will look after you very well, so let them know if you have any pain. Sister, we'll leave an order for morphine to be given as needed.*'

When they went on to their next patient, sister left the screens in place, drew up the straight-backed chair beside the bed and quietly talked with Tom for a long time, holding his hand. Alice learned so much from emotionally compassionate nurses like her; how to be with patients when they needed it, and when they didn't, and she took these fine examples with her into her own life as a nurse and midwife.

Alice wasn't there on duty when Tom died a couple of weeks

later, but before then she always spent an extra few minute with him when they were doing four-hourly 'back rounds'—rubbing pressure-sites with surgical spirit and putting on talcum powder to prevent bed sores—a practice abandoned a few years later as ineffective but at the time was a large part of the personal-care that Alice and her fellow nurses practised religiously. It was most often the physical contact between nurse and patient that was the benefit, not the spirit-rub and talcum powder, and Alice actually missed it for this reason when it was scientifically proved to be of little use as a preventative measure against bed-sores.

Caring for bed-sores (decubitus ulcers they were called in the patient's notes), was never easy. Not long into her training days, Alice was assigned to the task of doing the dressings on the ward for that shift. As students, they all knew, having practised many times with metal forceps in each hand, how to take hold of a cotton wool-swab and dip it into some cleansing or disinfectant solution at the start of the procedure The trick was then to rotate one's hands in opposite directions, squeeze the excess liquid into a steel gallipot on the dressing-tray, and then use the wet swab to clean the wound from the inside to the outside, before discarding the soiled swab into a paper bag attached to the trolley at the bedside. This was all so easy in the classroom on a dummy—and after being practised again and again was beginning to become second nature—until Alice encountered her first stage 3 bed-sore to clean and dress.

Her patient was Mary, a middle-aged woman confined to bed with a debilitating neurological condition, which was now at the point of semi-paralysis. Alice read in her notes that Mary had been living at home, looked after by her youngest daughter for some time, before she started to develop bed-sores. At first, they had appeared as simple bruised areas acquired during her transfer from the wheel chair to her bed, her daughter thought, but which rapidly became large open sores before turning into craters exposing the muscles, tendon and bone beneath. The process of necrosis had begun for her, and the smell of rotting flesh in her room was not fully concealed by the open bottle of *Nil odor* on the bedside table. Alice later came to associate this smell with necrotic wounds and calling it the *smell of death* in her mind she would never use it if she could help it. On this occasion, she was grateful for it, and wearing her cloth mask she set about her task to dress Mary's wounds. She soon realised that Mary had no sense of pain in her back and probably had no idea how extensive her bed-sore was—although she would have been able to smell it Alice was sure—but she was aware of Alice's touch and thanked her for her gentleness and for talking to her while she worked, cleaning with EUSOL (Edinburgh University solution of lime), which would help remove the dead tissue and encourage healing. Taking great care not to make the ulcer bleed, Alice wiped away the debris from the oozing wound, and then packed the gaping hole with moist gauze and covered it with overlapping strips of Sleek waterproof dressing, just as they had been taught. It would need to be dressed again on the next shift, but without the benefit of an up-to-date nursing-care plan (nurses didn't do much forward planning for patient care in those days), there was no guarantee that the same dressing would be used the next time. Alice began to wonder about the treatment of extensive sores like this. Preventative care was only a 'buzz-phrase' then but she was around on the ward when several treatments were tried on Mary's wound. A young doctor, early in his hospital residency, suggested oxygen therapy that he had read about. Oxygen from a bedside cylinder was directed through a rubber tube onto the wound for ten minutes at a time which was time consuming for the nurses but not without some benefit, everyone thought. But the next treatment he suggested was to apply honey—ordinary, everyday 'on-your-toast' honey—to the crater (which was measured every day and the size recorded in the patient's history), and then to pack it loosely with moistened gauze. He had read that evidence of this treatment had been found in Egyptian mummy's from over five thousand years ago, which Alice found totally amazing. Historically, mouldy bread, Alice read later, had also been used from time to time, and maggots too, to clean the wound, but she was most interested in the honey treatment and when it was ordered she used a wooden spatula to smear it carefully into the sore. But it was all to no avail, the crater never diminished in size. Despite everything that was done for her, Mary's sacral bedsore (and others that developed on her hips because in an effort to keep her off her back she had to be nursed side to side), went to the next stage, and she was taken home to her daughter in an ambulance, with a bag full of NHS dressings and a promised visit by the district nurse, to spend her last days with her family.

Alice soon began to grasp that her rosy-view of life, health and healing would not be fostered by her idealism, because there could not be a *rosy-view* for many people—and she began to wonder about the *prevention* of disease as a special interest for her to follow. The sad truth, she thought to herself, was that there were no oracles, no saviours, and she became increasingly sceptical about the health profession's ability to heal and cure. She was on the cusp of understanding so much; on the tip of an epiphany, and she didn't know where it would take her—if anywhere at all.

Alice had noticed with pleasure, in the days before he died, that Tom's sores were healing despite his decrepitude, his hazy blue eyes smiled at her, and that he looked peaceful. He had no visitors; there were no relatives to be informed of his death and he was given a pauper's funeral—partly subsidised by the hospitals' benevolent fund and the local council—which was arranged by the almoner.

Alice knew that she wouldn't need a pauper's funeral like Tom, and in fact she had already arranged for her body to be donated to a university for research purposes, if all the conditions worked out, but she often mulled over her increasingly reclusive life and how it might impact her and her family in the end. She had her last will in place and also an *Advanced Directive* which spelled out her end-of-life requests but she was becoming acutely aware that she would need help to have her dying requests met—she wryly added *'help at the end'* to her list of 'needs' to be met—along with mantelpiece dusting, fridge emptying and window cleaning! She could still laugh at herself, and she liked that!

She put her more weighty thoughts behind her for the time-being and with her memory awoken by thoughts of Tom at St Helen's she returned to her writing task knowing full well that she had much, much more to tell.

CHAPTER ELEVEN
And What's More...

In her fourth and final year Alice was assigned as a staff-nurse on a surgical ward, and worked hard to establish her place there, but she was burdened, unhappy, she was fractious, her duties, including staff-rostering and directing students were onerous, and it showed. And she knew it showed.

She began dating a man who was older than her who had a lovely sports car—possibly the only thing that she had on her mind when she said 'yes' to a drive down to Brighton to take in the sea air—but it wasn't a match made in heaven, just like none of her relationships had been—and she was contemplating an early release from her obligatory fourth year of her training so that she could fly away to the other side of the world before Christmas, thereby breaking her contract and preventing her from officially graduating. An early departure would enable her to spend time with her family in Australia for their first Christmas together for quite a few years. It seemed to her to be a really good idea at the time. An escape. And escape she did—*she flew away to the antipodes like a common sandpiper*, she liked to joke!

She felt she had a future ahead of her once she had settled in her life in Australia—a new life in a new country. There was a great deal to settle into, too. Australia seemed to her to be like a reflection of the 1940s that she had seen in early films from the USA. Milk bars, a bit like American drug-stores, but not as cosy as the corner shops she knew when she was growing up, were a ubiquitous pleasure, and very convenient for small purchases such as milk and bread and 'lollies' and 'icy-poles' on sunny, hot days, with the wide canopies they called verandahs, overhanging their windows giving shade and making them so easy to identify along a busy street. Australia's currency had not long since been decimalised and she found that her first challenge—making change—was anathema to her and she avoided it at all costs. She found herself handing over bank notes rather than have to work out coins, not unlike the way she felt when she first visited some of the South Asian countries that she came to enjoy later in her life—her purse was always overloaded with small change!

Alice found a job at the local hospital, on the general ward—a mixture of surgical and medical patients—and set-to learning the new terminology she heard all around her: 'counterpanes and bed covers' were 'quilts', and the top sheets were turned in under them, not precisely placed 18 inches over the top of the bed cover as they had been trained to do; 'cotton flannels' were 'face washers', 'vests' were 'singlets' and doctors came in from home in their suits and ties, yes, but no white coats, and joy of joys, nurses wore easy-care white dresses with white shoes and sheer panty-hose, still with white caps on their heads though, but no aprons and no fancy belt buckles.. and they worked many hours less than Alice had ever known. Forty hours a week! It all seemed like a holiday, it was so relaxed and friendly.

Jack followed her out to Australia a few months later after his mother died, and they resumed their relationship. But why did she get married that same year? She actually couldn't make sense of it to herself for some time. But it was done; she had made her bed and she must lie on it she knew, and the next thing she knew they was expecting their first baby. One of the senior nurses on her ward who came to her wedding (Alice only knew people she worked with at the time so they were all invited to join in her wedding celebration), advised her not to get pregnant because she had a good career ahead of her, but it was too late. She had been married just a few months.

She was made for motherhood she knew, not only because she conceived so easily, but she loved being pregnant like her mother had before her. Alice learned everything she could about childbirth: breathing techniques for labour, breastfeeding, baby care and, in those days before internet searches, she frequented the local library and bookshops in search of all knowledge about this new phase in her life. Later, in her thirties, when she started her midwifery training, she was surprised at how much knowledge she had accumulated along the way. Alice had a hankering to be a midwife from the very first time she saw the happy group of nurses on the trainee-midwives table in the dining room at St Helens, who would be called to the 'phone in the middle of a meal and then excitedly rush back to their department in full flight throwing on their capes as they left. Midwifery was still a mystery to Alice that she wanted to solve and understand and be a part of—and a lot happened to her before she did eventually achieve her wish. But there are other stories still to be told.

CHAPTER TWELVE
Alice Learning about Alice

There was often sadness in everyday life at St Helens, but the greatest sadness seemed to Alice to be the many men, women and children living with what to her seemed to be a living death. One patient in particular who moved her deeply was a young woman, just in her early thirties, with severe rheumatoid arthritis. To touch her, to help her turn in the bed, to give her the everyday nursing care that Alice and her fellow students were learning to give, was so exquisitely painful to her that she was beyond crying out, beyond sound—she just opened her mouth wide in a silent scream more articulate than any other form of expression.

Alice learned here on this ward, that this was not the osteo-arthritis that she herself was to experience in later life causing her to wake with painful knees and which made walking difficult sometimes until she warmed up to the exercise—this was rheumatoid arthritis which made limbs like those of a rubber doll; malleable; without form and structure; abnormally flexible; without muscle mass and resistance. Alice couldn't remember this patient's name as she began to write about her so she called her 'Sophie' in her mind. She recalled the feeling of her flaccid limbs as she carefully washed her using the basin of water on the bed-table beside her and a soapy flannel, and then rinsed her body with warm water from a second bowl. They had been taught to make sure that every patient had privacy and warmth before beginning a bed-bath routine and to follow the procedure systematically beginning with the face and ending with the genital area, carefully drying every part after rinsing the soap away with a separate flannel. But what Alice had not been taught when she first encountered Sophie was how to interact with a patient who, to Alice, seemed to be trapped in a useless body.

Sophie was in hospital waiting for hip surgery which wasn't going to make any difference to her physical ability but was hoped to reduce her pain in the long run. *'Long run'* was a stupid term to use, there was no long run for Sophie, and she was a problem to look after; she was irritable and contrary; compared one nurse against another, often with vitriol; and she needed help with every activity; turning over, sitting up, eating and using a bed-pan. She had a beautiful face with soft, soft skin, maybe due to the cortisone treatment that she was given, but she had such a mean nature that Alice thought soon that would show on her face. Alice wanted to not have to care for her—and noticed that Sophie felt the same way about her, too. Alice knew that she lacked the skills to *'jolly her along'* as she saw some other nurses do and she felt inadequate so many times with her and dreaded having to answer Sophie's call-bell.

This was major surgery that Sophie was going to undergo, and everyone wished her well when they wheeled her bed out to the corridor on the way to theatre. Normally a patient would have been transferred to a trolley, leaving the bed behind for the staff to prepare for their return, but Sophie wasn't going to be returning to this ward and Alice felt momentarily guilty as she breathed a sigh of some relief at this news. There was no doubt that everyone wanted Sophie's life to be bettered in some way, but sadly in those days, those times, the treatment was very little different to that of today, although medications have improved. Alice thought of her friend Jenny from her teenage days who told her that she thought she would develop the same debilitating condition, just as her father had before her. She had no contact with Jenny after she visited her just once at St Helens (she was the only visitor that ever came and sat in the nurses' sitting room with Alice), but she had only come to ask Alice if she knew anyone who could help her obtain an abortion (which was still illegal in England at that time), but when she realised that Alice wasn't able to help her, she left. They never saw each other again, although Alice wondered about her often, and also how rheumatoid arthritis had affected her life. Jenny was resourceful and would have sorted out her unwanted pregnancy sensibly; Alice was quite sure about that, but an autoimmune disorder was less easy to deal with, and she felt a great deal of sympathy for her when she saw how it had affected Sophie.

Alice had so much she wanted and sometimes needed to share. She was very dependent on her nursing colleagues for this, and her friend Monica became a reliable sounding board. Alice had Jack as her boyfriend, but she was very conscious of the fact that she couldn't share these things with him. She knew she couldn't describe to him how she felt about what she saw and was touched by, or even tell him about Jenny's visit, so she didn't try. Even though she had the insight to know that this was an 'amber flag warning' in their relationship, she still didn't do anything about it. It was better to have a boyfriend than not have one, she thought far too often. They went to the cinema, took trips down to the south coast on nice days when he wagged off work, and went to football matches and the pub with his friends. But they didn't talk about anything that really mattered.

So, it was inevitable that she would be attracted to someone who asked her questions, who was interested in the work she did and her feelings about it. Philip was having a gap year, as it came to be called, working as a hospital porter while giving some thought to what he really wanted to do—Alice knew how that felt from the time before she chose nursing. He was interested in a teaching career he said. He played the trumpet in a jazz band and he liked to dance wildly and he was fun, and Alice was smitten. He wrote beautiful prose and poems for her and sent them to her hospital address for her to find in her pigeon hole which she checked every day just in case there was a blue aerogramme from Australia waiting for her there, and just in case there was another love-missive from him. It was all addictive and self-affirming, she knew, and she savoured it all.

Philip was living in a small, one-room flat, twenty minutes' walk from the hospital in one of the beautiful old brick houses that had been subdivided into as many rentable rooms as any greedy landlord could manage. Alice visited him there often when he wasn't working at the hospital, or at his second part-time job as a life-guard at the local swimming pool. His family had a farm in the west country and his mother and his little sister came to visit him once when Alice was there, but there was no friendly connection at all between them. Alice was hurt at the time but she came to see that his mother had the sense to know that Phillip was no more suited to her that Jack was. She did none of the things that Phillip was interested in and although she could be interested enough to go along for support, and even accompany him to secret 'Ban the Bomb' meetings in someone's house, she knew that she was not the right person for him. She thought she was 'in love' and was very upset when the relationship faded and she worried that she would never find anyone to be her 'rock and stay'—with a Mother who liked her—and, in truth, she never did find a mother who liked her, but she did find love much later in her life when she thought it would never happen.

CHAPTER THIRTEEN
Some Things Are Meant to Be

She had been writing all evening, hardly moving, wrapped up in her thoughts and her memories of times past and of people, many of them since '*passed*'. That was not a word she ever liked to use, like '*gone to heaven*' and '*to eternal rest*' it was not what people did as far as she was concerned, and she was always straight to the point in correcting them if she heard those words used. She used the words *dying, death, died* instead with the pragmatism that was so etched into her nature, and she often received surprised looks if she took people to task on their use of euphemistic words and phrases in their description of the end of a life. If she didn't correct them audibly, she certainly did so in her mind. *No wonder*, she thought ruefully to herself sometimes, *that I have been alone for so long*!' She was not exactly friendless but she was not 'surrounded by family and friends' as was often said in press notices advising of someone's 'demise'—that was an acceptable word to use she agreed, but really 'death' would have sufficed. She did smile to herself to recognise that she was pedantic in this; she was rarely without self-deprecating humour, and was rarely sad, even when she thought of many of her encounters with death and dying during her career. She certainly wasn't morbid in her thoughts; she always knew that birth and death were a beginning and an end, and that both should be given the chance to be the best of best experiences in their own right, whenever this was possible. It was what she strove to do as a midwife and felt disappointed if she wasn't able to provide the best experience for the mothers in her care for whatever reason. She was saddened to hear of premature and sudden unexpected deaths too, and she always hoped for minimal suffering and an opportunity to be part of her own dying experience when the time came…well that was her hope, anyway.

She eased herself up from her chair pulling slowly up on her rope and noted that this was becoming harder for her to do with each passing day. Her back ached and she switched on the lamp on her chair-side table to find her Panadol tablets in their foil blister pack. She had always refused to use a tablet box—a dosette—dispensed by a chemist with daily pills placed into little compartments one for each day and time of the day. It seemed demeaning to her that she might not remember to take tablets that were prescribed but she didn't have many to take, really—just a daily aspirin and Vitamins D and B12. She refused to take anything else, and had refused for some years, but she was beginning to think that she might have to reconsider this as her ankle swelling increased—despite the dandelion leaves and asparagus her hairdresser had recommended for her to take—as she became more breathless with simple exertion, and as her heart seemed to flutter from time to time causing her to stop and rest. The signs were there that her health was deteriorating and she knew she would soon need to ask for help. She would call the medical centre for an appointment in the next few days—she really would, she told herself—but she was busy, she had to get her thoughts down, her memories imprinted on paper and relieve her ever full and fitful mind.

After so many years of fierce independence the idea of giving herself over to medical intervention was abhorrent to her. As was the idea that she might just need some assistance with daily chores—so she set herself the task of sorting the fridge, clearing the out-of-date items into a large plastic bag for Edna to dispose of when she came the next time. Edna had a key to her house and her next-door neighbour, Effie, had one too. She also had their contact numbers in her smart-phone should she ever be in need of them urgently—not something she ever envisaged, but just in case. She prepared herself a snack of a soft-cheese sandwich on whole-meal bread, and took her plate and mug of white tea back to her living room to see the last of the evening light disappear from her windows.

She was never fearful of the dark or of being on her own at night, not now, although there was a time in her life when she *was* afraid, when her heart beat so hard in her chest that it hurt, when she startled at every noise, imagining footfall on the gravel drive outside her window and she was afraid to go to sleep and lay with a knife under her pillow. This was when she was alone in the big, empty house after her marriage ended and her family had fled. She remembered being so afraid one night that she called an out-of-hours medical clinic number just to talk to someone on the switch-board. She never told the kind operator that she was afraid of being alone: no, she told him the truth—she said that she was troubled by the way her life was and she didn't know how to cope with the loneliness and her fears for the future. The language skills of the 'phone operator in Dubai that night didn't stretch far enough to include any counselling platitudes, but his tolerance in just listening to her offload her worries helped get her through that night. She eventually worked past her fears and her anger and got on with her life, making herself busier and busier, filling in time and her future, making a life for herself, pushing boundaries for herself and, in the process, pushing herself away from the life she knew she truly would have liked to have—which was one of being surrounded by friends and family... and never know what loneliness was.

Jack had walked out on their marriage; Jack had failed— not the marriage, she thought often to herself in the early days of their separation, until she came to see that she was party to this failure. He didn't just leave because he had found someone prettier and younger and more likely to give him the loving comfort he craved—and help him look after his two boys—but Alice knew she had driven him away, never stopping, always planning, always working, always busy taking on projects to fill her life with, which Jack couldn't be a part of, and which left her with no time to be a 'true Mother' to their boys. And in the end, she didn't need Jack for any kind of fulfillment in her life. And he didn't want her—not for anything at all.

After their second baby son was born in Australia, Jack became restless and wanted to go back to England—he missed his life there he said, and his friends too, and Alice knew he missed the social life he had had with them. Perhaps, Alice considered in reflection of their parting, he might even have thought that a move back to their familiar territory, where he was happier, where she was happier and more fulfilled, would bring them closer together: Alice's origins were British like his, and she had British ways about her, and British tastes after all, didn't she? But he didn't know her or what she needed—not really.

Alice had completed her midwifery training in Australia before her second pregnancy and she thought they were quite settled in this beautiful country. She loved the day-to-day pleasure of helping women in labour and birth too, even though it was hard for her to imagine that she would only be a part-time midwife for the foreseeable future while the boys were growing up. She had wanted to give more of herself to her career and she contemplated leaving him to go on his own back to England. But her boys needed their father, she thought, and she couldn't envisage a life on her own with them; bringing them up as a single mother when she had so much, she wanted to still achieve for herself, would be too difficult—so she went along with Jack's plan. They packed-up and left, flew away, saying dry-eyed goodbyes to her family and the few friends they had made, at a farewell party on the beach one summer's evening in suburban Melbourne.

That was the last time she saw her parents, that afternoon on the beach. Both had died before she came back to Australia years later when her life had changed yet again. She had been notified by her youngest brother about the circumstances of their deaths: 'from natural causes—age related' the message said, and she was sad at the news but not inclined to travel to mourn with a family she hardly knew any more. Her siblings had travelled far and wide and settled in many different places of the world—falling in love and partnering with residents of those countries. There were Christmas cards exchanged for a while after she left Australia, but many were returned marked, 'not at this address', and even email addresses bounced back as 'undeliverable' after a while. *Well, that's that*, she mused one Saturday afternoon in the back garden, in the November sun, at her Melbourne home, when in a rare moment of solicitude and nostalgia, she was about to address her Christmas charity cards when she realised, she had no addresses to send these cards to—no prior correspondence to refer to, and not even any current email addresses to use as a last resort. She placed the signed cards in their envelopes into a box, with all the many birthday and Christmas cards for her sons' that she had written, addressed and stamped but not sent, and returned the box to the hall cupboard, *in the dark where it belongs,* she thought to herself.

They had been living in England, settled in the south of London for a couple of years, when Jack came home one day saying he had a job offer to move to Dubai. To say that this came as a surprise to Alice would have been an understatement, but it was more than that—his lack of communication about his plans, his sheer lack of thought and consideration for her needs or even a basic understanding of what her own work meant to her—boiled up and blended into an angry bubble inside her that sowed a bed of resentment that wouldn't go away—it just grew and grew.

But she still moved with him, loyally trying to share in the excitement that her boys were feeling in anticipation of their big adventure in the Middle East. She packed up their house ready for rental, leaving her chintz-covered lounge-suite behind and taking just her pink-upholstered antique chair and its wooden foot stool and a few of her favourite paintings and ornaments with them. As part of her meticulous forward-planning, she arranged for a suitable English-speaking school for the boys to attend in Dubai, spoke with the headmaster by 'phone, and sent their last term reports by fax from the local post-office to the admissions officer of the school. A furnished home would be provided for them as part of the 'job package' which included an allowance for a cook and a cleaner for their residence which was in a locked and secure compound twenty-five minutes' drive from Dubai central. It all seemed very slick and straightforward, and she started to warm to the idea of this move. She investigated work opportunities for herself—she would need something to occupy her after all, she thought—she was like that, always needing a project, a work commitment, to feel fulfilled. Tennis and mahjong groups were not enough for her to fill her time and keep her active mentally and physically; she had always worked, given something of herself to her community, learned and gained satisfaction from her work. It was just the way it was. They quarrelled often about this before they left. Jack argued that she had no need to work, he could provide for her and they would be expected to be social with the other ex-patriots in their new community—and she looked at him in disbelieve that he couldn't see that what he was saying, what he was suggesting, was loathsome to her.

She had never wanted her family to be itinerant, moving and travelling like she had to as a child of an air-force family; no, she wanted to give them the security of a home for them to come to, where they knew they were based—a real home with familiar things around them.

She started to lose her sons, not just her husband, when they went to Dubai. She changed, she was seething inside; she became remote and disconnected from the world she was in. She found the heat unbearable, despite her teenage years having been spent in a similar climate she could not acclimatise, and she spent much of their first few weeks there indoors, in air-conditioning. She hated that people were in her house cleaning and cooking and doing the things she wanted to do and, in her miserable mental state, she soon discharged them. She hated the lack of any freedom she had to roam, to investigate, to sit and observe and to wander alone in her thoughts and dreams in the outdoors and on a beach—there was a guard at the compound's gate who checked her in and out. And she hated the attractive and cheerful young women from many cultures in their strapless sundresses, with tanned shoulders who, as solicitous neighbours, knocked on her door offering welcome-gifts and invitations. They soon stopped trying to engage with her and invitations to soirees and fund-raising events stopped coming through the door. Their sons were invited to parties and sleep-overs, and appeared to be happy in this largely manufactured and over-heated place. She dropped them off and picked them up from magnificent chalk-white homes in palatial grounds, often greeted at the door by meticulously-attired staff in long kandura robes and wearing the Arab headdress, the kaffiyeh. She never ventured further than the doors of these places, never stopped to chat, to make small talk. And so, little by little, she isolated herself from their society, and in her doing so, compromised Jack and his position in their expat environment. And the most awful thing, she saw in herself, was that she didn't care.

Eventually she was offered work that Jack had found for her, teaching English to the young children of a wealthy family who lived in a palatial apartment block with a magnificent view over the waterfront, which was a salve to her soul for a time. She enrolled in an Arab language class where she was accepted just for herself, and she started to soften, to come to terms with her lot in life, but she knew she was damaged; her marriage was damaged and her relationship with her sons would never be the same again.

When Jack left her, he took her boys, and they went willingly, secure in the knowledge that *Dad* wouldn't let them down, embarrass them in social situations, or leave them to fend for themselves while he wallowed in self-pity like their mother had done. Yes, indeed, Alice came to understand, Jack hadn't failed her, she had failed them all. She had failed herself.

Ironically, she thought to herself now as she wrote her story, all that planning, working, busy-ness, and constant need to learn and participate, had actually saved her life and brought her to this time in her life when her mind was still clear enough to become a dedicated writer in her old age. And she wouldn't have met Kelly if things had not worked out this way.

CHAPTER FOURTEEN
Some Things Are Meant to Be

Kelly was older than Alice by nine years but he still didn't need to die before her and she felt cheated by him—not in the way that Jack had cheated on her, but Kelly had given her the promise of forever love and support at their commitment ceremony in their beautiful back garden in Melbourne. On that glorious day Alice wore her emerald-green velvet dress with the Cinderella collar that she had secretly stored away, carefully wrapped in tissue paper: the same dress that she had always planned to wear at the re-enactment of her wedding vows with Jack, the day that she had visualised so clearly in her mind for many years—until Jack left her.

She has thrown out her reminders of Jack in the depth of her despair but she was surprised to realise that she had not thrown out this dress, and then she acknowledged to herself that this dress actually had nothing to do with him at all. The wedding re-enactment she envisaged had nothing to do with him either—it was to do with *her* vision of their life, *her* plans for the future, *her* expectations of him, and the promise she made to herself that the dress would still fit her well when the time came to wear it. Her vision was not that they would have reached their enactment ceremony in a marriage founded on love and respect and caring either, but only that when the time came, she would be proud to repeat her vows.

Wearing her dress that day, standing with Kelly, she finally felt like a grown-up woman, owning her mistakes and ready to commit herself fully to another person and she knew she glowed from the reflection in Kelly's eyes and the warmth of his kiss. But life was never meant to be easy for her it seemed. Nor for Kelly.

They travelled the world together; visited all the places in their retirement that they had always yearned to see, lacing their trips with laughter but relishing their return home to sit again peacefully beside a roaring fire in total and unreserved companionship together.

And then Kelly died; not a devastatingly sudden death as a car accident or a cardiac arrest from a coronary would have been, but a lingering, painful, agonising, tortuous loss of glorious life into an abyss of unpleasantness, ignominy, and withdrawal from reality. And Alice stayed with him, cared for him, became his nurse, no longer his muse, and she again raged inside at the unfairness of life and that this was happening to them now. This wasn't Kelly walking out like Jack had done, in one swift movement tearing away bonds and destroying memories as he went, it was a gradual thing, destructive and painful for them both to the end, and impossible to begin to come to terms with while he still breathed.

Alice was accustomed to recognising harbingers to the finality of death, to hearing fatal diagnoses spelled out to patients while they clutched hands with partners and family, but she had not totally understood the physicality of these moments for the participants in those tableaux. That clutching of hands she had seen so often as an observer, was replicated in her body and in her stomach making her feel nauseated, as the grey-haired specialist, looked down at his notes over his glasses and then consulted his computer screen before announcing that Kelly had less than six months to live: '...*caught too late, advanced too far, spread too far, treatment ineffective now, help with palliative care, pain relief, get your affairs in order, come back and see me in two weeks, any questions?*'

Of course, there were questions to ask, Alice knew all too well and she agonised over the lack of control they had at that medical appointment. *But who can ever remember to ask the right questions at that moment with blood pumping in your ears as the words that you never wanted to hear are spoken out loud? You just don't grasp it, you don't hear it, your mind races ahead to 'hospital or home?'* was what Alice wrote in her story about this time in her life. But on this day *who? why? where? and when?* were questions that consumed her as they drove home in silence. She touched Kelly's knee and this time there was no answering and comforting, responsive touch from his hand on hers as they had learned to do for each other. He was already leaving her.

Alice had nursed patients with late-diagnosed pancreatic cancer before and knew that the end would be painful, that she must summon all of her own emotional strength to help him in his extremis. But first she had to subdue her internal anger that this was happening to him, to them. She took herself away to a peaceful, private remote beach that she would often withdraw to, where she could rant and rave about life's unfairness, and there being no such thing as a kind god, and feel the pain of remorse at the absence of close family in their lives, people close enough to share her pain with. They would need to tell his children, if they could contact them, his siblings who were spread across the world like hers, and his friends (they had few mutual friends— the ones she could send Christmas cards to, signed *from Alice and Kelly, with love*—but Kelly had an old Moleskine notebook in his desk drawer with entries on every letter of the alphabet which she would have to go through with him to be sure she wasn't notifying long ago and distant contacts when he died. Kelly's last will would have to be revised and then they could settle to planning for the next few months.

And then she had to cry—she sobbed and bawled and pounded her fist against a tree until her knuckles bled and then she became calm, and didn't cry again until the amorphous shape of the Kelly person she once knew lay on their bed that she had vacated to distance herself from being his lover to become his nurse. She watched through his last hours as his spirit left him and considered as she had often done in the past, just where does that spirit—that life force—go at death? She sometimes wished that she could believe in a higher being, a god with a heaven, hell or purgatory for the soul, but that belief, that faith, wouldn't come to her; she saw that he was gone, his eyes told her even before she felt his pulse fade and his breath become shallow. He had gone into himself and was not there for her ever again. Then she climbed onto the bed beside his cold and wasted frame and repeated the words she had spoken prophetically to him at their commitment ceremony—*death may part us, but it will never take away our memories.* Then she got on with her life once more, in the efficient manner which she had learned.

CHAPTER FIFTEEN
Connections and Disconnections

Alice had lost contact with the surviving members of her nursing intake and had not seen them since a reunion event fifty years later when they were largely unrecognisable to each other. Some names were familiar but the people they had all become had somehow given them masks, some reflecting the lives they had lived. Lian who had been an early friend at the hospital was there with Jharna but they had nothing in common with the young women Alice knew. Lian was clearly a heavy smoker and showing the ravages of a life-time of nicotine use, and Alice remembered how a group of them would congregate in one or other of their rooms, sprawl across the bed, still in uniform, or squat on the floor playing cards, with cigarette smoke thick in the air. She had conversations that reunion day with several of her peers who needed prompts to recognise who she was, but Alice had remembered most of them and the part they played in her early nursing life and was fascinated to hear stories of their many and varied achievements. She remembered, with some amusement, back to a time when a small group of them had gone to a ten-pin bowling alley for a rare evening out when one of them felt sick. They all watched like stunned-mullets while the poor unfortunate one vomited into the toilet until Alice stepped in and held her hair back and used her own head scarf to wipe her face and clean up around the bowl. Alice was always practical and thoughtful but not always sure of herself and she knew her self-esteem wasn't high so when the group praised her for acting like a 'real-nurse' on this occasion she felt enormously pleased to be acknowledged by them.

She heard stories at the gathering of travels as missionaries, feats of organisational skill and bravery in the face of terrorism in London, and the establishment of enterprising businesses to provide palliative home-care in countries far afield. She looked around the now very mature group at their reunion on that sunny English day, and she thought to herself: *No, no one is just anybody… no one is ever just a nurse.*

She asked about her friend Monica who she had lost contact with many years before. They had exchanged Christmas cards, with brief letters enclosed, for a couple of years after Alice had moved to Australia, and before she moved back to England with Jack. They just didn't seem to have anything in common after their training days ended and they moved into their nursing careers. The last she had heard was that Monica was engaged and about to be married and her mother whom Alice finally met briefly before she left England, had died, but the host of the re-union told her quietly that Monica was now 'in care' after she developed Alzheimer's disease and no one had any other information about her. '*Sad*', Alice said to her, '*after we shared so much*', and she wondered if Monica would have recognised her had she been able to be there that day. Alice knew she would have recognised Monica.

CHAPTER SIXTEEN
Telling Tales

Sleep was elusive to Alice in her dotage. This inconvenience wasn't new to her; she had spent many a long night in her life in restless tossing and turning waiting for the wave of weariness to take her over into slumber; this sleepless state wasn't like that now; it was useful and productive time when her thoughts came already ordered and purposeful. She needed to write: she needed to be out of her bed and into the dim light of her sitting room, the shutters still open but filtering the night sky and giving her some privacy from late-night dog-walkers and casual passers-by.

*There was no 'social media' in my young day*s, she wrote, *that entertained and informed and sometimes shocked and could be shared with friends when they were particularly interesting or contained a video that amused. No memes.* But then she thought more about this statement and came to the conclusion that they actually hadn't any need for such explicit and artificial communication at St Helens—they had each other, and each other's stories, tall-tales and funny episodes to share and sometimes laugh about, and so many others to cry about. Many of these sometimes visual, sometimes acted out, and sometimes whispered narratives and accounts had stayed in her mind's recesses and she could recall them clearly.

Monica once told everyone at tea-time, the story of a patient in the casualty department who was brought in late one evening—twilight-time in England which seemed to stretch forever, before night finally won and took over. A middle-aged woman from the local community brought her elderly mother in for a medical assessment of her mental state. She was showing signs of confusion, she told the staff, her short-term memory was amiss, and she hadn't recognised her daughter when she called in to see her that day. During the fairly lengthy wait to see the doctor, the old lady was placed in a cubicle on a trolley with her daughter sitting on a tall stool beside her; both were weary, and the daughter was very concerned that by the time they were seen her mother would be worse. Finally, a doctor, a junior resident, pulled back the curtains and came to stand beside his assigned patient. He was a kindly young man, dressed in the manner of all his superiors in a suit and tie and a white coat with ballpoint pens, and a fountain pen for writing prescriptions for the hospital pharmacy, showing out of his pocket. His notes would later be written in ball-point ink on the un-lined foolscap paper in a named folder held in the office filing cabinet; only his medical notes that is—nursing notes would be written in a separate Kardex for handing over to the next in-coming shift, each version telling a separate side, an alternate tale, about the same patient. The two versions, as a composite document, would be considered to be 'holistic' in today's terminology, Alice supposed, but back then the two versions were quite discrete; although nurses would read the doctors notes, rarely did a doctor read a nurse's notes. And nurses' notes were not kept for inclusion in the history which would later be stored in the patient records department.

However, this evening the young doctor introduced himself to both mother and daughter then asked a few questions about the purpose of their visit to the hospital and listened to the daughter's answers while observing her mother. 'Now,' he said to the old lady, 'I just want to ask you a few questions to see how you are doing. What's this?' he asked indicating the teacup on the side table. And then, 'what's this?' pointing to the chair in the cubicle. 'and this?' he asked, holding back the sleeve of his white coat.

'That's a wrist-watch,' she said. The old lady answered everything she was asked correctly, although with a little more hesitation each time she responded—until he held up his necktie to show her.

'What's this, dear?' he asked her. She paused, leaning forward to touch his tie, lifting it up and feeling the fabric with her fingers. She took a long time to answer while her daughter looked on in dismay at her not knowing such an obvious item of clothing. Her lack of response seemed to be substantiating what she suspected—that her mother was heading for, if not already suffering, senile dementia.

At long last, the old lady looked up at the doctor and answered, 'It could be rayon, but I think it's polyester.' And then she lay contentedly back on her pillow having done everything that was asked of her. They were home within half an hour, delighted with the outcome of their visit and leaving a happy little tale to be shared around in the sitting room!

The best story teller amongst them was Pauline who had mistaken Alice's father for her chauffeur when they arrived on that first day, which now seemed to be so very long ago. Pauline could engage an audience without any difficulty, she could imitate voices and 'did' accents cleverly and her rendition of Australian slang was both funny and astute, and she was often asked for an encore just so they could laugh out loud which they loved and sought every opportunity to do—they found very early in their training that laughter was wonderfully therapeutic. But Pauline could also be irreverent and mischievous and although they knew they shouldn't be amused always, everyone thought it was hilarious when she said: '*Stand and Deliver!*' to a pregnant patient who had a suture inserted as a new treatment for an incompetent cervix, as she was helping her to get out of bed for the first time after her surgery!

Pauline was a complex person, Alice knew, and in the way of many people who are humorous, used comedy to attract, to explain, and as a coping tool. And she was also promiscuous. She was one of the few who started relationships with doctors in this teaching hospital, visiting them in their annex rooms at night. Although she was quite discreet about her adventures and no one knew who she had liaised with, the word was that she was 'out there'. Alice reminisced that most of the new nurses had crushes on the young doctors from time to time. Alice never did, although she quite liked the young resident who thought that honey would be a good treatment for bedsores, but he was painfully shy she remembered. By and large the housemen and resident doctors were a good-looking crew, outgoing and a similar age to the nursing-students and most were unattached, so it wasn't surprising that they were sought after.

Pauline had a way about her, and she was smart, well-bred, attractive and, funny too. She spent the rare times when holidays were available during their training, to go skiing in the Swiss Alps with her mother, her step-father and her older brother. Her parents had divorced when she was quite young and although she rarely talked at length about that time, she had said that she found the whole experience devastating, the fights between her parents, the financial constraints put on them all and the recriminations of 'fault' that had to be proven, were not only distressing but, as she said, embarrassing. She had been sent away to boarding school on the south coast of England to protect her from some of the upsetting events, but then had to leave because the school fees were prohibitive, but it was here at school, separated from her family that she developed her humour, her skills in entertaining, and also some sporting prowess which made her an interesting companion for the men she dated. Alice always regretted that she hadn't had the opportunity to go to boarding school herself in her teens, but although not a fatalist and always a practical reasoner, she came to the conclusion that she had had many opportunities in life that others had not and she was glad about that. From time to time, she did wonder how she might have fared in her own relationships if she had Pauline's confidence and opportunities in life, but she had shared her sense of humour and enjoyed some happy times in her company and that was enough.

Black humour was an everyday, useful commodity for the first few years of their training, until they became staff-nurses and each put on the mantle of maturity with their registration as 'bona-fide' nurses. In her fourth year Alice knew that she no longer could use this humour as the crutch it had been, though sometimes laughter bubbled up from nowhere and often inappropriately. It was, however a useful concealer for feelings that were too hard to express, and helped cushion so much of what they saw and heard and smelled. She had a last vivid memory of inappropriate laughter in her student days when one night she was helping Monica attend to a frail old German gentleman who had gas-gangrene in both legs. One leg had already been amputated and the other was badly disfigured with black dry skin worn away to expose the bone. The smell was horrendous, raw—that sickening smell of rotting flesh—and invasive in the small room he had been isolated in. They wore nurses' gowns and masks and gloves which they had donned before entering the room to attend to this patient, and took up their places, one on each side of the bed. One carefully washed him and other dried him and together they helped him into a clean hospital gown, and remade the bed with clean sheets and covers. He was barely aware of them as they ministered to his needs and as they were placing the bed-cradle over his leg, Alice said quietly and seriously to Monica, '*One day we'll find this leg in the bed.*' There was something in Alice's dead-pan delivery of this factual information in the still of the room that made Monica's eyes widen above her mask as she stared at Alice, and the second that Alice noticed her reaction she felt the rush of mirth in her throat that she knew she would not be able to control and she left the room to double up with laughter in the corridor, with Monica close behind her. It took them some time to compose themselves enough to be able to return to their chore and complete the care that they had nearly finished, all the time stifling their inclination to laugh out loud each time they thought about it. They remembered this occasion again and again and could never work out what it really was that amused them so much that night. In the end they concluded that it was black-humour, that escapist humour that made so many things bearable for them—although it never fully masked the sights and smells of their experiences or helped them to be wiped from an everlasting, and in many ways, unforgiving memory, it was still their salvation.

CHAPTER SEVENTEEN
Beginnings and Endings

Alice had met Kelly twice in her life but had totally missed the opportunity and the joy of knowing him the first time around. He had been a patient on the medical ward at St Helens in the third year of her training just after her theatre rotation, and on her first shift she was responsible for handing out the medications. Another shift member, a second-year student, was preparing the injections in the clinical room while Alice was pushing the medicine trolley along the ward and stopping at the end of every bed to check her list and compare it with a chart hanging over the bottom of each bed frame. When her colleague came to join her with the tray of injections, they would go together to a patient who needed assistance to turn over for their injection, drawing the curtains around the bed to give privacy. All intramuscular (IM) injections were given in the buttocks then, high up in the right-hand quadrant, to avoid the sciatic nerve as they had been taught. The 'safe spot' could be located by drawing an imaginary cross on the buttock with a swab moistened in spirit, and they were very diligent in this practice so as not to cause unnecessary injury, paralysis even. Years later when it was considered safer to give injections into the muscle on the thigh, Alice still preferred to give IM needles 'the old way' because the patient was less likely to tense up in nervous anticipation. They had practised and practised in the classroom, injecting into oranges, trying to get not just the injection right, but also how they prepared the patient for it, reassuring them with the right words and making them comfortable. Still, when the moment came for their first time, they were all in trepidation. '*I did it!*' they proudly announced afterwards in the dining room and everyone knew what they meant.

This particular day—the day she met Kelly for the first time—she had gone to help give an analgesic injection to a cancer patient in the ward and then returned to her trolley and as she moved on, she heard a voice from behind her. '*Hey, you missed me, am I too late? Shall I jump up on the cart!*' These words, taken from Lonnie Donegan's song *My Old Man's a Dustman,* made everyone smile in recognition of the lyrics in those days and she was already smiling when she turned around to see Kelly, his eyes shining in humour with a quizzical lift of his right eyebrow. He was taller than her, but not by much she noted, and older than her too, but not by much either she thought; she saw these things, taking in everything about him in a moment; he was quite slim, almost thin, she saw. His hair was dark brown, later to turn a beautiful, clean grey, but she saw that he had lines around his mouth, unhappy lines which disappeared as he slowly smiled at her and the crease between his eyebrows softened too, giving him a younger face. She might have been fanciful enough to think she fell in love with Kelly at that moment, but she was a nurse, a nurse on duty and she had her duty to perform. '*Well, I wouldn't have missed you if you had been in bed where you should be!*' she bantered as professionally as she could muster, but with a smile too.

Kelly was being investigated for a gastric ulcer and had told his doctor that he had a gnawing pain in his stomach which went away for a while after he ate, but his constant indigestion left him feeling nauseated most of the time, and he was a smoker as indeed Alice and most of the people she knew then were. She also learnt from his medical notes that she read later in the shift, that Kelly was indeed older than her by a several years and had a very stressful job as a journalist on a well-known London newspaper. He had assignments overseas on a regular basis and he was married with two small children.

Alice wasn't surprised to read about his marital status; anyone so charming and good looking was bound to be attached, she had decided long ago, but she was surprised that he already had children and resolved straight away that she should avoid him whenever possible. She knew that she never wanted to be involved with a married man—infidelity was so wrong she believed and she didn't ever want to be implicated in that. So, she did try to avoid him. That evening she had to change his milk-drip bottle which he was being given to settle his symptoms and hopefully help relieve his pain and aid in the diagnosis by differentiating the cause of it. As she moved around his bed, she saw him looking at her and they exchanged smiles, *and that*, she said to herself ruefully, *is that*. He was moved to another ward the next day following a review by the surgical team.

In the 1960s it was still common belief that peptic ulcers—stomach and duodenal—were caused mostly by stress which was thought to cause the excess of acid in the stomach which eroded the lining of the digestive tract and without the aid and benefit of many of the tests that Alice came to see performed and perfected, it was a matter of ruling out all possibilities. No one at that time stopped Kelly from smoking, but later—much later—Alice supported him in stopping his habit, but the damage had been done.

All patients' beds had ashtrays in their bed-side lockers and Alice had herself lit a cigarette for someone who was in the habit of using a nicotine smoke to get their bowels moving, or was depressed, or tearful or anxious. It was curious, for Alice looking back, that somehow, they didn't notice the smell of cigarette smoke in the air, even in the cinema when the haze above the screen was so obvious, nor the unpleasantness of emptying an overloaded ashtray, and in fact at that time, patients weren't even asked about their smoking history. It was a fact of life, but as Alice and the world found out, it was also a fact of death.

So, Kelly's treatment initially was a milk-drip administered throughout the night via a tube in his nose into his stomach which both fed him and was intended to soothe his pain, when it was suspected that his ulcer was bleeding.

Alice reflected often and sadly, that if only the bacteria Helicobacter pylori had been discovered before 1982, and the medical profession had recognised its role in peptic ulcer disease, Kelly may just may not have had so many problems and surgeries and suffered the pain he did. He had constant revisits to hospital including for a vagotomy to reduce stomach acid, partial gastrectomy, peritonitis and ongoing gastric problems for all of his life. But Alice didn't know about all that then she just saw him as a peacefully sleeping patient after their smile exchange, lying on his back with the rubber tube in his nose attached to a bottle, with its contents glowing ghostly white in the light from the window.

They next met over thirty years later when he was a patient in her ward in the Victorian regional hospital where she was a charge-nurse. She was helping out her staff during the busy afternoon admissions session. She felt no immediate recognition though there seemed to be something familiar about him when she greeted him. It wasn't until she was attaching his identity-armband to his wrist, checking that the name was correct and corresponded with the name on his history, that she looked up to see him looking at her with a memorable enquiring glance and lift of his eyebrow. He was being admitted for a revision of abdominal scar tissue, she saw from the next day's operations list, and as she was filling out the paperwork with him, they sat on either side of her office desk facing each other. She asking him all the usual prescribed questions: name, age, marital status (divorced, he said). He watched her eyes and mouth as she spoke to him, listening to her voice, with his head on one side, which she was later to learn was due to deafness caused by a sojourn late in the Vietnam War when a bomb exploded near him killing his friend and effectively putting an end to his journalistic career. She had so many proscribed questions she wanted to ask which would have been unacceptable in this professional working space, and she felt herself flushing, too acutely aware of him. She wanted to ask: *Who are you now? What career have you taken up? What happened to your marriage, your wife, your children?* In her fluster she brought the interview to a close quickly, opened the door into the corridor and asked the ward-clerk in a room opposite to take Kelly to his bed in the ward. As he passed her in the open doorway he whispered in the words of Lonnie Donegan and with a smile in his voice, '*You missed me? Am I too late? Can I jump up on your cart?*' And with that brief encounter, life was never the same for her—or for him.

Six weeks later she had given in her notice, cleared her desk, accepted a farewell tea party from her staff and had flown to Vietnam with Kelly—while her beautiful Melbourne house was being refurbished for them.

Kelly had become a published writer after his time in Vietnam and he was lovingly generous in sharing his skills and knowledge with Alice. He taught her how to collate her notes, how to embellish her short stories creatively, use the editing keys and thesaurus on her laptop and—*show don't tell,* he advised her firmly! And she thrived in her new obsession—she was beginning to write her stories properly and she had so many stories to tell.

No relationship that Alice had ever seen or known was without its difficulties, without its dissents which would leave both parties pained and often full of sorrow, wanting to be gone, threatening to be gone, sometimes going. If there was violence it wasn't always physical, sometimes it was verbal, cleverly inflicted wounds with words made to create the lesions that once spoken were almost impossible to heal. With Kelly she had arguments of this kind, the small disagreement that flared without warning into a deluge of insults and abuse without either of them ever knowing or understanding where it had sprung from. On one of these occasions when they argued—in a trivial way at first over whether the fire should be lit before or after dinner—the dispute escalated to the point of no return and the impact of his words to her and hers to him caused a breach that seemed to be the end for them. Alice walked out with only her handbag and her backpack, which still contained some personal items for overnight travel from their last trip away. He didn't try to stop her. He sat fuming at his desk with his back to her, unforgiving and angry, and let her go.

Alice's pain was so acute, she felt horribly sick as she drove the car away from him as far as she could go, and as fast as she could. She had to run from his anger and from his words. She didn't cry, not then, but she was determined that she would not go back to him, not after all that they had shouted at each other, faces twisted in anger. So, she stayed away a week—she went to Bendigo but didn't confide in any of her friends there—she booked into the Shamrock Hotel and walked the park and streets and created in her mind the way she would tell him that they were finished, ended, done. She would not be treated like that, nor spoken to in that way every again, nor be provoked to say the things she had said. She had no sorrow for her part in the argument, not for her words, because she knew that she had spoken honestly, just not as gently as she might have wished, and she would not accept an apology from him either because he, too, had spoken the truth about their relationship.

When Alice finally arrived home, he wasn't there, the house was empty—but didn't feel empty, it felt warm and comforting and the fire was blazing in the sitting room. On the low table by the window with her pink-chair in front of it, Kelly's lap-top was turned on and open with a glass of wine on a drink-mat beside it. She sat down and read what she knew he had left there for her to read.

To Alice, who has rendered so many of my days perplexed or intolerable—

But so many more once so happy
Who has left a scent on my life and left the walls
Dancing over and over with your shadow
Whose hair is twined in all my waterfalls
And hours littered with remembered kisses.

So, I am glad
That life contains you with your moods and moments
More shifting and more transient than I had
Yet thought of as being integral to beauty;
Whose mind is like the wind on a sea of wheat,
Whose eyes are candour

To whom I send my thanks
That the air had become like shot silk, the streets music.

So that if now alone
I must pursue this life
You are the one I always shall remember
Whom want can never corrupt
Nor argument disinherit
Smiling like a diamond in the wind
Frowning as a would-be angry mother
And taking enormous notice of hats and backchat—how could I asses
The thing that makes you different
You whom I remember glad or tired
Smiling in drink or scintillating anger
Inappropriately desired.

Sometimes untidy, often elegant
So easily hurt, so readily responsive
To whom a trifle could be an irritant
Or could be balm and manna
Whose words would tumble over each other and pelt
From pure excitement.
Whose fingers curl and melt
When you are friendly.

I shall always remember you in bed with bright
Eyes or in a teashop stirring coffee abstractedly
And I shall always remember how your words could hurt
Because they were so honest
And even your eyes were able to assert

Integrity of purpose.
And it is on the strength of knowing you
I reckon generous feeling more important (than ever I did before).

Then the mere deliberating what to do
When neither the pros nor cons affect the pulses.
And though I have suffered from your special strength
Who never flatter for points nor fake responses,
I should be proud if I could evolve at length
An equal thrust and pattern.

I am too harassed by my familiar devils,
By those I cannot see, by those I may not touch;
Knowing perfectly well in my mind, on paper,
How wasteful and absurd
Are personal fixations, but yet the pulse keeps humming
And your voice is heard
Through walls and walls of indifference and abstraction
And across the rooftops.

And my common-sense cries 'fool'
And my pride, in the name of reason, tells me to cut my losses
And call it a day, which if I had the cowardice of my convictions
I should try to do
But you melted my amour, and mortally wounded me
So do not expect a wounded man to walk from the field so bravely
As one who never knew the battle
And was never hurt.

Of a sudden I see you sleeping gently
And you think that I ought to hate you
But since I don't, will try to make me
Save your trouble for I could not
Hate you, for your instinct
Sanctions all you do.
Who know that truth is nothing in abstraction,
That action makes both wish and principle true;
Whose changes have the logic of a prism
Whose moods create,
Who never lingers, haggling on the threshold
To weigh the pros and cons until it is too late.
At times intractable, virulent, hypocritical
With a bitter tongue,
At times all woman, warm and soft
In the climate of love,
Embracing with the fury of a tigress
With the gentleness of a kitten.

You are all around me, in me, of me,
Now—as you were then,
Quick to sound the chimes of delicate intuition, at times malicious
And so generous at times.
Whose kaleidoscope ways are all authentic
Whose truth if not of a statement, but of a dance
So that even when you deceive, your deceits are merely
Technical and of no significance.

And so, when I think of you, I have to see you,
In thought and on your own ground;
To apply to you my harsh canons

Would merely be unsound.
You say you are not perfect;
Did I ever ask you to be?
Just human—which you are,
Beyond any person I have ever known.
So, if I die sad at my loss
I die happily at my gain, having known you

So, you with whom I chanced an idyll,
Sleep, there, elsewhere, places I can no longer enjoy,
And wake to a glitter of dew, eye-shining sun and to birdsong.
And you whose eyes are green whose ways are foam
Sleep quiet and smiling
And do not hanker for the perfection which can never come.

And you, whose minutes patter
To crowd your social hours
Curl up easy in a placid corner
And let your thoughts close in like flowers.

He came to stand behind her as she read his poem on the screen, and then she turned to see him and both of them in tears, they came together in an embrace. Alice never quarrelled with him again, because she knew that he truly understood her.

Their time together was well used. They talked and dreamed, wandered and loved, and dreamed of where they would go; they explored the best places to wander and they loved each other both gently and passionately. And Alice, who hadn't prayed since she was a little girl learning her catechism, prayed that this would be their life forever.

CHAPTER EIGHTEEN
Alice and Kelly

There were occasional blimps, of course; life isn't without blimps they both knew, but these blimps mainly resolved themselves. The biggest blimp for each of them was their children. Kelly's family were living on the south coast of England all within close range of each other. His two boys were now married with children of their own but they had estranged themselves from him after the divorce which they blamed him for, and in truth Kelly could see their reasoning. He had been a stranger even to himself when he came back from the Vietnam War, he didn't want to engage with anyone, least of all anyone who made demands and certainly not the demands his wife made on him. She wanted him to slip into the old-slippers of marriage and the life of the village where they had settled, help renovate the cottage with a view to selling it so they could move on to something bigger and better with the proceeds, and in the meantime pop up to London for a weekend of theatre and fine-dining occasionally. He couldn't see himself in that life anymore and then there wasn't the money for it either His prestigious career as a journalist was over and although his writing fulfilled him at a deeply personal level, it did not fulfill his role as a wage-earner and provider. The boys would have to leave their private schools, he told his wife, and she would have to go back to her modelling career for them to keep subscribing to this lifestyle. There were angry rows where his harsh voice filled the house and frightened his children, and they wished for him to be away from there following his career in overseas places—or anywhere else except there—and to leave their mother alone. One night he came home after drinking with his friends (his only friends, he realised), to yet another argument and found the next term's school fees waiting on the kitchen table for him to see. As he once again, tried to explain to his wife that they couldn't afford the privilege of a private school education for their sons, she flew at him, scratching his face and using her full open-handed force to hit his head again and again, he used all his strength to hold her back and looked into her face seeing the dislike and wild-eyed anger there and knew it was all over. He walked out of the cottage with a feeling of release, and never went back. She had his clothes and personal belongings sent on to him via his solicitor's address. Once the divorce-nisi for dissolution of their marriage came through and the cottage was sold with his half interest paid out to him, he took himself off to Phu Quoc to write and earn himself a living from articles and short stories to magazines. He never went back to England, and he never heard from his ex-wife again, nor his sons or grandchildren, though near the very end of his life, he would hallucinate and talk about them with Alice as if he had just returned from a family visit. He would describe the lovely time they had on the beach, playing cricket (he let them win, he said, pretending to catch them out, then dropping the tennis ball at the last moment), and everyone went paddling in the shallows, he told her, searching for shells washed into the pools in the rocks until the dark clouds started to roll in from the south and they scuttled for home. Alice wasn't in these stories he imagined, she knew that, and when he was recounting them, he held her hand with his eyes shut. She always hated that he sometimes shut his eyes when they were making love and she knew he was back in his imagination with his wife in her place in his bed, or worse, someone else from his past. She never said that to him; she never told him about how she felt usurped by his previous life on occasions because she was a realist—she said to herself—and it wasn't feasible that anyone could totally erase a memory, especially powerful memories like the smell and feel and touch of intimacy with another. Still, her heart felt her pain. She knew he loved her in his way, he didn't need to tell her—he was there with her, wasn't he? They laughed together, missed each other if one was gone for any length of time and they were joyful in their love-making when they were back together again, but she always knew that she was his second choice, his second chance. When he lay in their bed, close to his death, he withdrew first from Alice before his mind withdrew altogether, and in those moments, as she patiently watched his spirit leave, she had wondered where he was in his thoughts. Now, as she wrote her story, sitting on her own in the warmth and light and familiarity of her little sitting room in the house she had purchased and they had together filled with memories, she knew where he had been—and it wasn't with her.

CHAPTER NINETEEN
To Thine Own Self Be True

Dawn came: never as wonderful as the red glow of an Australian sunset in her mind—it was on the wrong side of her house for this; however, dawn had become a most favourite part of her day because it came without the connotations of a departing, an ending, an encroaching darkness. But this day's dawn brought another reality to her life. Another kind of dawning. Finally, she truly felt herself to be alone, she understood her aloneness, she embraced it, and although she had been alone for many years, now she knew that this was what she wanted, and what she chose.

In a clarifying moment of epiphany, she came to understand many things including that her children had not abandoned her, they had just wanted another kind of parent, another kind of parenting that she could not give, and it was what Kelly's children had wanted from him too, all those years ago. She understood why they kept themselves away, withdrawing by degrees and without clear notice and concealed themselves from her in their lives and their families. Without any of the formality of a goodbye, they took their leave of her with an irrevocability that she had no wish to try to overcome. They were in their early thirties when they last had any contact with her and she had been in her fifties.

Her sons hadn't liked Kelly from the outset and she had seen this in their subtle avoidance, with paper thin excuses, of any invitations Alice extended to them after they had met him at their commitment ceremony. Their questions about him made it clear that they saw him as an imposter—a charlatan—pursuing Alice for her money and her home. On the occasions when they had been in his company, they would not engage with him and if he tried to engage with them they responded with an undisguised put-down, a not-so-subtle disparaging quip or jibe, which they were both very good at—*learned from their father*, Alice used to tell Kelly when they talked about it. She couldn't understand why they were so resentful of the time she spent in travel with Kelly, rarely asking about where they were going or when they would be back and there was an undertone of concern that Alice was funding their combined lifestyle. And she was. But she reasoned that that was none of their business; they could just be accepting of her choices in life.

Alice's sons had brought their wives and little children to the happy commitment ceremony in the garden, and at first both boys seemed to be almost relieved that Alice had someone to be with, to share her life with, but very soon it was clear to Alice from their gradual withdrawal that they were less than comfortable with Kelly sharing her life so profoundly, and her home so proprietarily. *So be it*, Alice thought to herself, I will always have him, always be true to him above all others until death do us part; and she dismissed their concerns summarily. *If they cared at all about me, they would still engage with me even if they didn't want Kelly in their lives,* was her mantra which she espoused, with a metaphorical toss of her head. She still found criticism as hard to take now in the late part of her life as she had when she was a child, and through every life-stage in between, but she didn't care quite so much now. But all this was before Kelly died and before her life changed once again.

She was unaided in her care for Kelly at the end. After the

fatal diagnosis was told to them, they had briefly discussed contacting an assisted dying organisation, but in their research, they stumbled across the origin of the word *'euthanasia'* meaning 'a good death'. A 'good death' would be the goal they would strive for; rather than have another person, or people, intruding into their scant time together. Kelly told her that he trusted her to be always with him, make the right decisions for him, physically care for him and manage his dying process with kindness and wisdom. And she did, but it was not easy and it took its toll on her and when it was over, she took some time to come up for air—to recover enough to re-engage with her world—but she knew that she had followed her dictum *'to thine own self be true'*. She had been true to herself, and she always would be.

She received cards from both her sons, signed by their respective wives, expressing their condolences at this sad time, and addressed to 'Mum' but not mentioning Kelly by name. Their cards were still on the mantelpiece when she returned from her month-long trip to Queensland in search of healing, soothing sunshine where she had 'railed against the wind'; fighting, cursing and reviling death as a worthless adversary, and ranting at the unfairness of life once again. That he had let himself be taken away from her, was a recurring theme in her head, day and night, until she acknowledged that she was blaming him, making him personally responsible for this outcome, and she knew she had to take charge of herself again

She moved herself into the small second bedroom at the side of the house the week after she got back—it was adjacent to the kitchen and closer to the sitting room she reasoned, but in truth she had given up their bedroom to him in his dying—she no longer could rest there, she could only sleep fitfully with vivid dreams waking her far too often even when she took the sedation that Doctor John had left for her (along with a repeat prescription), when he came to place his stethoscope on Kelly's chest in the hours after he died. She left Kelly's clothes in his wardrobe to deal with on another day, and shutting the door behind her, she set about planning the next stage of her life.

CHAPTER TWENTY
Acceptance

Kelly, she came to realise, had given her with the greatest gift of all gifts—the tools and confidence to write. To express herself in words, to collect from her mind the events of her life and create a cohesive story around them, and to keep her memories fresh for further plucking, gave her so much joy and occupied most of her days, and many of her nights.

Alice wondered where her acceptance of her solitary life had come from, when it had come, and she paused in her writing this day to gaze out of the window watching early morning clouds clearing and sunlight taking over the sky. She had been transcribing her foolscap notes on to her laptop sitting in her canvas director's chair at the scrubbed timber table in the kitchen, when a message at the top of her screen came through advertising the benefits of Vitamin D and she was immediately transposed to another time in her life when she had become aware of the role for vitamins and minerals in health.

She wasn't, and never had been, a health fanatic. She ate meat and loved it. She used real, hard, 'just out of the fridge' butter in her cooking; and relished the often defamed 'English Breakfast', and fried egg and bacon was always a favourite for her at weekends when she gave over her morning to a leisurely meal and the crossword in the Saturday paper. She ate well, but not extravagantly, maintaining the same weight she had when she first met Kelly—his coming to live with her had become the reference point for her for so many things; *how old was next door's cat when Kelly came? What year did Kelly arrive? Did Kelly help me plant this tree?* If she had voiced these thoughts aloud to a would-be listener, she might have seemed somewhat boring, a little obsessed even, but she was neither of these things. She did however sometimes require triggers, rebounding platforms even, to allow her memories to spring forward to take over and help her create her stories. The mention of vitamins was one of those triggers.

As a nurse on the orthopaedic ward at St Helen's she had handed out calcium and vitamin tablets to fracture patients, she remembered, but she had no idea at the time what they were really, or what they actually did. She understood that calcium was necessary for healthy bone growth, but the benefits of the vitamins was not part of her limited but growing knowledge-base. Much later she understood that sunlight was essential too, and she wondered why all patients were not encouraged to be outside in the fresh air like the patients in the TB ward at St Helens, and when *Methicillin Resistant* S*taph. Aureus* (MRSA) became a phrase that just slipped off the tongue and then into the consciousness of all hospital staff—and created fear in the community—she wondered why sunlight wasn't used to augment other treatments. So cheap and so accessible, she thought.

When Alice was working briefly in a general practice in Melbourne, before she took up her role on the surgical ward where she had met Kelly again, she researched the use and important role of Vitamin D in everyday life and it became her little pet project for a while, and she wrote about it in newsletters for the patients, and spoke often to her colleagues about it not being so much a Vitamin but more a hormone with its regulatory role in stabilising calcium and maintaining a healthy immune system. She resented that she was advised to keep out of sunlight because of her fair English skin, but Alice was never one to bow to undue pressure to do anything—including avoid the one thing she liked to do best! She loved nothing more than to feel sunlight on her skin, to lie on a beach listening to waves lapping behind her and hearing the sound of happy, family groups playing and chattering. She did not need to be alone there on the sand, and if she was, she was not so peaceful—she was watchful and too aware of her surroundings. She was mindful of her health in her maturity, and of her mental health, and she always knew that she felt most well when she had been in the sun, spent time at a beach walking or lazing, and this day at her kitchen table she knew she needed sunlight.

Her garden, her constant pleasure, had gone to seed in the years since Kelly had left their home, and she needed to stir herself to do something about it. Her need for sunlight took her outside in baby-steps—first to sit and raise her face to the warmth of the sun, and then to the garden shed to find her secateurs and gloves. She walked back from the bottom of the garden and placed her tools on the wrought iron table where they had so often sat sipping their evening wine from freezer-chilled glasses, in comfortable companionship talking about the events of the day, or planning trips to come.

I have no heart to do this now, she thought, and as the word 'heart' came to her, she glanced down at her legs, noticing how swollen they were, mottled and puffed with her ankles spilling over the sides of her light canvas shoes. *Vitamin D will not save me now!* her thoughts continued drolly, *and I must hurry to finish my story—my tales—so I leave nothing unfinished, nothing left unsaid.*

She had been sitting at the kitchen table for some time before venturing out through the French-doors out into the garden but when she came back, leaving the door open to the summer's afternoon, she went straight to her chair in the sitting-room where she had begun her writing journey, and where she could raise her legs with her feet on her stool and help ease the fluid accumulating in her lower legs. She had planned to make an appointment to see her doctor, but put it off once and then off again. Alice didn't think he had been very supportive when Kelly was so sick, reluctant to make house calls until the very end when he came to pronounce him dead, and left her to call the funeral home when she was ready—which she did, many hours later. The last time she had seen Doctor John before that was a week earlier when he had left a prescription for morphine in liquid form to give Kelly if it was needed, and told her that if it became necessary, he would be back to give him morphine by injection. She often said to Kelly that this doctor had no empathy, he was dismissive of any of her concerns leaving her feeling foolish for having raised them, but she had bought her house in that area in the years of singleness before she had Kelly, because she could walk to everything, she needed including the medical centre, so she kept him as her '*sometimes and only when necessary*' doctor.

The small-shop owners in The Strip had become her friends; they called her by her first name and always greeted her with a kindly smile. She knew enough about each of them, their families—and their politics—to joke that she could write a book about them. She never would, they were just a special part of her life there, and she marvelled at how they ran their businesses, day after day, always solicitous, always ensuring that their customers moved-on down the street feeling cared about. Her hairdresser, Zoe, on the block was the one that knew the most about her; not just the right shampoo to use and which colour to use to blend with her increasingly greying hair, but where she preferred to sit, when she didn't feel like talking, when she was absorbed with the deterioration in Kelly's health and when she was becoming breathless herself as her own health was compromised. Without asking her she positioned Alice with the basin-chair nearly upright to wash her hair and didn't take her time over a head massage which she knew Alice had enjoyed in the past. Alice wished this kind of service was available from her doctor, without the head-massage of course, but as it wasn't, she delayed visits and avoided contact with him. He once sent a nurse to visit her for an 'Aged Assessment', but the sweet and earnest young thing asked Alice to identify three objects and remember what they were a few minutes later, and then count backwards, and tell her the date, month and year, and who the prime-minister was (*who cares*, thought Alice, *and anyone could be excused for not knowing given the frequency with which Australians swapped them around*), all of which she had found quite demeaning. She had no problem with her memory, nor her cognition and she would never develop senile dementia she was certain of that. She just craved intelligent conversation with caring people and if an opportunity to talk about her writing came up, it was even better. She had no feedback on the aged assessment when she next saw Doctor John for a 'flu vaccination; therefore, she assumed that she had 'passed' the test!

It had been difficult for them in Kelly's last days without compassionate support from any close source, but they managed together. They didn't need or want anyone in their world but they accepted the daily reassuring visit from the palliative care worker from a city hospital in his last days. Now, with all that behind her—sorted and done—it was becoming apparent that she would need some help soon for herself.

CHAPTER TWENTY-ONE
So Much to Do, So Much to Say

Alice slept in her chair, her head resting on its curved, firmly-padded back. She wasn't very tall, just a comfortable height to be able to walk with Kelly's arm around her shoulders in the days when they checked out tourist sites in countries they visited. They had walked the streets of old cities and got lost in the ancient medina of Fez in Morocco, and so many other places that were a joy to experience in their travels together. She felt that she was becoming shorter—diminishing with age, because her head still felt comfortable enough in her chair, but she had to bring her foot stool closer to her before she settled, with her black cashmere-throw over her knees, so she could rest and let sleep waves overcome her. Before she dozed, she had tumbling thoughts in her head about the other things that were happening to her as her aged.

She seemed to have become invisible, discounted by people in the street, in the shops—other than her own neighbourhood merchants that is. Groups coming towards her in the street appeared not to see her and she had to move aside to let them pass; and this happened far too often to be coincidental, she was well aware. She considered always using a walking stick so that she could hold it out in front to bring attention to herself, but perhaps she just needed to be vocal—*'Hey, I was here first!'*— she sometimes wanted to call out in the queues where she was ignored, but she hadn't wanted to bring that degree of attention to herself, she just wanted to be acknowledged.

She woke to the sound of her door-bell in the hallway and heard a key in the lock, and, at first disorientated about the source of this disturbance to her sleep, she roused herself sufficiently to call out to her visitor that she was on her way. It took her some time to disentangle from her throw-cover and bring herself up to standing. She thought momentarily that one of those wheelie-walker things that she had refused at the aged-care assessor's suggestion might be quite useful in situations like this. She didn't get many callers—not many people who rang her door bell—legitimately that is—but although it was approaching evening it was still quite light, and she didn't hesitate to go to the door.

Her neighbour, Effie, was one of the two people who had a duplicate of her door key, and she was someone whom she engaged with on a regular basis. She was not just her neighbour, she was her friend and she loved her. Effie looked concerned, her face appearing around the door before Alice fully opened it to welcome her in. '*I heard noise in your garden-shed early today,*' *she told her, 'and then nothing, I didn't hear no other sounds, no gardening going on, so I just come to say hello and make sure you all right.*' Her Italian accent had all but disappeared after so many years in Australia—she arrived the same year Alice first arrived—but not her manner of speaking, the literal translation of her thoughts and the phrasing which Alice always thought was delightful to hear. She might once have called it 'bad English' but not now; now she was enchanted by it. They had sometimes talked about whether Effie dreamed in Italian or English and Effie confessed that she still thought of herself as Italian although she sometimes dreamed in English. Alice on the other hand thought of herself as Australian—Alice, Kelly, Effie and her husband, Joe, had all been become naturalised Australians in the local Town Hall ceremony on the same Sunday afternoon in January many years before. Sometimes Alice looked around at her furnishings and arrangement of her house which were distinctly British, even to her own eye, and some of her sayings and mannerisms and her attention to social niceties were hangovers from the old country she knew. But she felt proudly Australian just the same.

Effie came into the house and immediately, chattering to Alice as she went, took herself to the kitchen, emptying the contents of her basket of fruits and vegetables from her shop onto the bench and into the fridge, and then put the kettle on to make them both a cup of tea. Effie took everything in; she was a very clever person Alice knew and she would have understood immediately. She would have noted Alice's swollen legs, her breathlessness as she greeted her at the door and the greyish pallor of her skin, the lack of order in the house, the strewn papers from her writing on the kitchen table and the open French doors letting in a strengthening, cooling-breeze threatening to blow her papers onto the floor. She would not comment, not Effie—she wasn't like that and she was not a fusser—but she was concerned, and was of a mind to intervene, recognising that for the very first time since she had known her, that Alice—independent, self-managing and determined Alice—needed help.

Alice would have no bar of this. She was not about to have her plans disrupted and was ready to stand her ground... all this without a word having been exchanged between them about what was apparent to them both. They talked common trivialities, Alice remarked she hadn't seen their cat in a while and Effie told her that the old thing just liked to sit in the sun these days and wasn't interested in climbing fences in search of kindly stroking, '*a bit like you and me, eh?*' she asked! And they laughed at this comment with its element of truth about habits and needs in older age. Alice explained that she had gone out to start some overdue gardening but then changed her mind and came in to have a little sleep instead. She told Effie about her plans for an early dinner (she still called it dinner, in the English way, regardless of the time of evening she ate it), and after their cup of tea at the kitchen table she asked Effie if she had a good recipe for her to concoct a meal from the vegetables that she had brought for her. Alice, without prompting, told her that she was booking a visit with her doctor soon to talk to him about her swelling legs and reassured her that they were looking a lot better now that she had had a nice rest with her feet up. She thanked Effie for popping over and for her concern and, asked her if she would take the plastic bag of out-of-date produce from her fridge that she had left in the kitchen for Edna to dispose of and put it into the bin, and as quickly as she could politely do so, showed her to the door.

She returned to the kitchen with a disconcerting feeling of having been 'sprung', Effie was 'on to her', pre-empting her plans, she was sure—she needed to speed up and finish the job, finish what she had started, before there was too much interference. She had loose ends to attend to, many words to write still, papers to organise and preparations to make. No time for delay.

CHAPTER TWENTY-TWO
Always a Dreamer; Always a Planner

She had bought this house, this house of her dreams, after the Dubai sojourn. Once Jack's job at the plumbing consultancy was complete, without any further ado or any communication with her, he booked flights for himself, his Danish lover (Alice had suspected but hadn't known for sure), and their two boys, and was bound for London secreting the flight tickets and passports away at his office until just a couple of days before they left. She was grateful that he didn't try to pretend to her that he was only taking the boys for a holiday in the UK for a couple of weeks, although it would have been easy for him to do that given that she didn't bother about his comings and goings, and they had for some time lead quite separate lives—'separated under the same roof' their solicitor called it which would speed up divorce proceedings for them, should that occur, he wrote from England, with matter of fact delivery and impersonal legalese.

Alice felt that in some way Jack's sketchy plans to go 'home' after his work wrapped up that he told her about briefly in the weeks before his departure, would not be right for her anyway, and would somehow spoil England for her; *too close for comfort, best to make a clean break of it—let him go to England, sell the house, send her the proceeds due to her in due time and she could get on with her life—with her boys*—she thought all this to herself with never a word to Jack about her plans—instead she envisioned all the minute details of how she would head back to Australia and pick up where she had left her life there, bring her boys up in the warmth of the sun and the fun of the surf. She could provide for them, she was sure, she could work but still be there for them.

Alice came home from her language class that Tuesday afternoon to find an empty house, echoing with the voices she expected to hear but were no longer there, without any trace of her boys, their cupboards cleared out of all the precious articles of their boyhood, and her heart broke. She realised that she had not believed that he would go and take them with him—*he stole them!* She screamed at the void. And she blamed him, cursed him, that her life had ended up like this. In her total self-denial, and without the insight then to see the part she had played in this outcome, she felt powerless, incapable of rational thought and '*my life has been violated, I have been robbed!*' she screamed over and over again. She curled herself up into the foetal position facing away from the invasive light and she stayed that way until her emotions were spent, and the night came, and went, and dawn entered the room. She was beyond crying, beyond feeling, not wanting to be here, or to be anywhere at all in this world, with a pain inside that nothing could make better and where her inner thoughts was all she had to cling to.

The boys (once they had been *their* boys, then *her* boys before the time they became *his* boys) had their own passports which she had always kept safe, tied together with hers in her own office drawer in an envelope marked 'confidential' where their school reports and birth records were, for the two years they lived in this place. When she saw that their passports and birth certificates were gone, Alice fell into a renewed episode of reality-grief and she had no way of comforting herself; and there was no one there to comfort her. She was alone, lonely, emotionally bereft and devastatingly sad that she had let them all walk out on her.

    She booked the next flight from Dubai she could get bound for Melbourne, not caring about the times of departure or arrival, packed a small suitcase, arranged by phone for her pink chair and little footstool to be transported to a storage facility until further notice. She would let them know where to send them sometime soon, she told the helpful proprietor. And she walked out of the house, without a second glance, when the taxi came for her.

CHAPTER TWENTY-THREE
Reality... Chapter and Verse

There was so much they learned and took away from the three years of their training and the final contractual staffing year at St Helens, but Alice was firmly of the belief that the most valuable thing she learned was to be aware: to have the emotional intelligence to know when and what to say—and what not to say—to put herself in another's place, another's shoes with empathy. One day on the surgical ward a woman, not a young woman, was being admitted and Alice watched her walk down the ward to her bed with the swaying gait of someone advanced in pregnancy and supporting her girth with both hands. She didn't look as if she was in labour, Alice knew what that looked like. The woman was dressed in a colourful smock, loose over her abdomen to below her knees, which was standard pregnancy wear in those days when pregnant bellies were discreetly covered, not proudly displayed, as they came to be in later years, with tightly fitting tee-shirts and tights. Alice didn't know then why she hesitated in smiling and greeting her cheerfully as she did with most patients: there was nothing in the woman's demeanour that suggested that this was not a happy time for her, instead Alice just quietly helped her get undressed and into a hospital gown, and brought a wooden foot-stool to help her climb into bed, and extra pillows to arrange behind her back. She didn't ask her any questions, or make any comments other than to introduce herself and show her where the call bell on its cord was and give her general information about the ward, and the woman seemed at ease with that. Alice left her, with the screens around the bed, and went to find the staff nurse who had brought her into the ward.

'She has a tumour in her uterus which is inoperable,' the staff nurse explained, *'she doesn't have very long to live, and people think she is pregnant and make inappropriate comments about her conceiving at her age. I'm sorry I didn't have the chance to explain that to you, but I knew you wouldn't have said anything to upset her, so thank you for that. I'll take over now and call the doctors to see her.'* Alice, at that moment, felt the special feeling of being respected as a thoughtful and sensitive nurse and she remembered forever that she should assess first, consider situations, and follow her instincts, not her first thoughts, before speaking or acting. And she was grateful that she found this out so early in her nursing career and it stood her in good stead in many aspects of her life. It didn't, however, bring her close and lasting friendships or easily connect her with people in her personal life. She was too circumspect, too wary of disclosing too much about herself until she was confident that she could trust her confidante. Monica was an exception to this; once they started to know each other they shared many of their thoughts and feelings about the events that took place in their hospital and in their lives.

Alice remembered that she had once shared what happened in the stairwell outside the medical ward at St Helens, and disclosed to Monica how she thought about that at the time. The memory came back to her as she set about putting her affairs in order in the comfort of her own home—making provision for the end of her own life in her own way.

There was an elderly Jewish gentleman whom she had

nursed several times as she moved from ward to ward in her training and had come to know quite well. She liked him for his humour and his intelligence and for the stories he told about his life when she bathed him or escorted him on his short walks around the ward. He had developed emphysema from his long-time smoking habit and was permanently attached to the oxygen supply in the blue tank standing beside his bed. He had only one daughter, he told Alice, who lived in Amsterdam and she had come to visit him just before his last admission to St Helens; her little picture on his locker in its blue and white Delft pottery frame intrigued Alice and she asked him about her. He told her that she was married to a Dutchman who ran an export business, and they had five children (which he rolled his eyes at in a disapproving way). She wouldn't have asked him many questions beyond courteous conversation, except that he seemed to want to talk; he clearly wanted to tell her about his wife who had died suddenly two years before from a heart attack, and he wanted to tell Alice about his early life too. He had escaped from war-torn Poland and had come to England to be a tailor—opening up a little shop in the High Street which had thrived. He said he never smoked in the shop because the smell clung to his fabrics, and he never allowed anyone into the shop if he could smell cigarettes on them. He was fastidious in that—and as a patient he was fastidious too—a gentleman who used the table napkin that every patient was offered, in the correct way at meal times. And he was very private in his dressing and undressing—accepting very little help with these activities. If he rang his call bell it was only to have his oxygen cylinder replaced, or to ask a nurse to escort him to the bathroom.

One night his body was found at the bottom of the stairwell outside the ward doors. No witness; no explanation; no indication of why; no oxygen cylinder nearby He was dressed in the clothes he had worn when he had been admitted, and the photo of his daughter, out of its frame, was found in the top pocket of his Tweed jacket.

There was an investigation and the verdict was suicide by a man with dementia. Alice had never thought that he had dementia in her interactions with him, but perhaps he was temporarily affected by a lack of oxygen on that night, she wondered—but then when she talked to Monica about it, she said she doubted that was the reason that he fell; she knew deep down that his fall was intentional and she actually marvelled at the bravery of this kind and sweet man to do such a lonely thing on his own. When Alice and Monica had cried together about all this, they used the black humour that they often did to bring them back to a better reality. *'He could have just waited for the lift!'* Monica said in a complaining way, and they laughed irreverently. Somehow, Alice knew, he would have laughed too if he had heard that.

CHAPTER TWENTY-FOUR
Coming Home

Alice boarded her plane late that night at Dubai Airport, after Jack had gone, with the early summer air still steaming off the desert. She had no feelings one way or another about leaving this place—no feelings about anything at all really—nor did she have any particular notions about where she was going. Her ticket said Melbourne (MEL), and that was sufficient for her, she would work out her next destination from there.

As fate would have it, and in the wonderful way that chance can sometimes lead to opportunity, her allocated window seat was beside a couple returning home from a holiday in Morocco. They had had a lengthy Dubai stopover and they were excited and relieved to actually be on their way again. Alice was really not interested in making conversation or engaging with them on the journey, but inevitably she had to squeeze past them both to go out to the aisle to move around or to freshen up in the bathroom—after queuing for an excessive amount of time on this busy flight. Settling back into her seat again on one of these occasions she asked the young woman, out of courtesy rather than interest, where they were headed for. She had no thought in her head that Bendigo might be a good place for her to settle, she was virtually homeless, without family, and also jobless, so the choices were endless and infinite, but as soon as she heard mention of the name, *Bendigo*, where she had once visited in search of good pottery, she took it firmly into her mind and in the remaining hours of the flight, she conjured up a life for herself there in that city. *She would look for work in the hospital in the midwifery department—it was a growing regional area and they would need midwives and they had a midwifery training school which she would like to be involved with.* She would stay overnight in Melbourne, in a hotel close to the railway station, Alice decided, and then take the train to Bendigo the next morning. She scribbled her plans into her notebook and was surprised to find that her spirits were lifting—she had a plan to follow and it was her *own* plan, not one contrived for her to follow with her feelings secondary to anyone else's. She asked the flight attendant passing with his cumbersome drinks-trolley, if she could please have a gin and tonic? She quietly toasted the couple beside her, then finished her drink and finally fell into a peaceful, dreamless sleep. She was going home.

Bendigo proved to be the right place for her to be. The city was interesting enough for her to enjoy on her days off from the hospital which had welcomed her to their midwifery department, and she was soon asked to help tutor the new group of trainee-midwives. She at last had her epaulettes and frilled cap—and respect for her seniority—and for the first time since her training days, also a true sense of belonging.

She rented a little brick house which had many beautiful Victorian period features including stained-glass panels in the timber front door which let coloured beams of light into the long hallway—and there were tessellated tiles on the front verandah which was just wide enough for a chair and small table. The house was not in good repair, but it was partly furnished and the rental was quite affordable for her, and she took refuge there at the end of her shifts at the hospital, sitting on the verandah watching a sunset, or taking in the morning sunshine before work, when she was on a late shift. She went regularly to the local library to use their new computers to begin to construct the written version of her life; to put into words all the thoughts she had running through her mind and recalling all that she had experienced. She took a few classes on the use of the *world wide web* which appeared to be taking over, and had the whole world literally in its web, and she booked a computer spot once a week at the library for her to research information and events when the facts had escaped her. She didn't just write her life-story here; she wrote stories of every kind and every subject and in many writing styles. She looked out of the library window one day and saw butterflies and wrote about them being deaf in a touching little story about the shortness of a butterfly's life and the beauty that they bring to the world in their short existence, and saved it on her USB devise to print out later. She was busy, she kept herself busy, and she was not lonely at all. She walked in the botanic gardens, and spent many hours in the art-gallery and she occasionally joined her fellow midwives in the town's historic pubs, for birthdays and special events. It was such a nice, orderly satisfying life, free of conflict.

Bendigo had everything that Alice needed at that time in her life. Her work was absorbing, and challenging at times, and with her new-found contentment she opened up to others and she gradually found friends—or they found her. Her colleagues respected her knowledge and her wisdom but some would comment to each other that they felt intimidated by her and her friends would have said about her—'*She isn't easy to know or get close to, and she might seem distant and often holds back in conversation and sharing, but when she is with her mothers and their partners, see how she becomes a part of their lives and they allow her in. We can all learn from her.*' She was a very good role model for her students and she enjoyed teaching them the skills in midwifery that she had acquired along the way.

Each mother was potentially special to Alice, they each had a story to tell and even if they didn't choose to share it immediately, Alice gave them the opportunity to do so with her warmth and caring. Sometimes there were hours and hours of a long labour when Alice had to be encouraging, never to let the mother become despondent when dilatation of the cervix was slow—that was not what she would have said, some words she never used, like 'slow labour', instead she would usually adopt positive words like 'moving on' and 'progressing' and occasionally 'nudging along gently', depending on Alice's assessment of her mother's tolerance level for light humour.

Humour was always a part of Alice that lightened her load and made life worth living, and although sometimes hidden in a mire of angst, as in her middle years, was still there to be called on when most needed. Her midwifery practice gave rise to humour as often as her nursing training had, though some of the events that gave rise to the best laughs were almost unrepeatable. It was a shared humour that drew her to the friends she made in Bendigo and endeared her to many of her workmates, and some of their shared experiences could only be found amusing in hindsight. It was a comment about *'watering the garden on a hot summer's evening with a gin and tonic'* that first brought her to the attention of her colleagues at the lunch table. when she quipped that it seemed an awful waste of a gin and tonic! Sometimes it was the simplest of things that made them laugh and brightened their day.

Alice and her student were assigned a four-bed room in the labour-ward one day shortly after she took up her position as tutor. This was where women in early labour, or those having been medically-induced with membranes ruptured and waiting for an infusion of Syntocinon to be started to '*get them going*', were admitted. This was not the way Alice liked her mothers' to start in labour—it too often heralded a sequence of events which was like watching a train heading for derailment, Alice thought—but sometimes it was inevitably the only course of action, for the safety of mother and baby, and she always did everything she could to keep her mothers' on track to a safe delivery. This particular day she saw with relief and amazement, and not just a little gratitude, how the laws of nature and the wonders of modern midwifery could align and she was so very thankful for the excellent training that she had received.

Genevieve had been admitted the night before in early labour with her first baby, membranes intact and contracting regularly—right on-course. Her young husband was with her and they were a charming couple. Kind and responsive to each other, happily enjoying this new experience and looking forward to being parents. They had no particular expectations, no 'birthing plan', but they knew quite a lot about childbirth and Alice could speak frankly with them and involve them in everything. A very good couple for her student to engage with and learn from.

This was just one of those days when things happen. There was neither rhyme nor reason why events escalated the way they did, and even in the aftermath along with relief that things worked out, there was still disbelief that these two events could coincide.

Mariama was brought up to the labour ward by the admitting staff on the midwifery ward as Alice was preparing a bed for her. She was a large, beautiful woman of African descent wearing a loose brightly-coloured caftan. She was someone the staff warmed to immediately, and her loud infectious laugh raised the spirits of everyone in ear-shot when she walked in. She was on her own, her husband was home minding the other children, and she was totally unconcerned about the upcoming process—'*bin there, dun that, dahlin'*—she told Alice as she was examining her for the first time—and the only time, as it turned out. She was in the very early stages of labour. Alice's vaginal examination revealed no dilatation beyond that expected of a multigravida, but the cervix was ready. Alice sent her off to the toilet to provide a urine sample for testing while she returned to Genevieve to complete her set of hourly observations. She had attached a monitor to measure contractions and confirmed that there was no vaginal discharge, when Alice became aware of a noise from the patients' toilet. There is a tell-tale guttural grunt that some women give as they are preparing to push a baby into the world, Alice knew from experience, and this is what she heard from Mariama. The toilet space was small, only sufficient room for a toilet, handbasin and a receptacle for soiled pads, and certainly not a space for a baby to be delivered in. But there it was, as Alice saw as she opened the door—a magnificent ten-pound baby boy lying in Mariama's arms and opening his mouth to give a lusty cry, as loud as Mariama's laugh from her place on the toilet seat. The tale of the 'instant 2 to 10cm's cervix' was legendary in no time and often used as a cautionary tale for any complacent midwife. Alice would often tell her students—never turn your back on a woman in labour!

But this day had only just begun for Alice. After she had helped the staff in cutting Mariama's baby's cord and collecting the placenta (which had also come away without any intervention), and they had taken mother and baby to be washed and checked, she returned to Genevieve. In the short time she had been away the electronic monitor had recorded several good contractions with a heart rate corresponding within reasonable bounds. Alice sat with her for the next twenty minutes feeling her contractions and reassuring her about the events that she had just heard. It was not uncommon for a foetal heart rate to dip, and monitors recorded every little change, but what Alice felt was the baby suddenly being very active and she listened with her Pinard stethoscope pressing against the tight flesh of Genevieve's abdomen to hear the heartbeat which was irregular. She quickly pulled the screen around her in preparation for an internal examination and pushed the emergency bell for assistance before putting on her sterile gloves and elbowing back the bedcovers. Genevieve's husband had gone outside to make a phone call to her family, but she asked the staff to call him back and get medical assistance immediately. Her examination found that the membranes had ruptured and the amniotic fluid was green tinged and she could feel the umbilical cord pulsating slowly beside the baby's head when she felt through the half open cervix. With no time to lose, Alice told Genevieve urgently to turn over and lie with her head down and bring her knees up to her chest—practically an impossible ask, but she did her best—while Alice climbed onto the bed and in the most difficult manoeuvre with her fingers still in position in the cervix, she held back the baby's head to avoid compression on the cord.

Sometimes, at this stage of a pregnancy, midwives and doctors are more inclined to call the baby, a 'foetus', but Alice never did that—to her, all mothers were having 'babies' once they became her patient in labour, and on this particular day the baby became the most important thing in the world to her as they were rushed to the operating theatre for a caesarean section with all hands-on deck—and Alice's fingers saving a little life.

The outcome that day was two baby boys, both alive and

well, two happy and grateful mothers, two stunned fathers, and several midwives exhausted at the end of their shift. There was much to talk about and learn about from these events and laugh about too, and Alice was reminded so often that you never know what a day will bring in nursing and midwifery—and she felt eternally thankful that she had followed the career that had chosen itself for her.

Mariama and Genevieve met in the special-care nursery where their babies were kept for observation following their unconventional arrivals into the world, and the two mothers became friends together—and part of Alice's friendship group too. They would all meet regularly at back-yard barbecues at one or another's house, and Alice would watch their children playing and remember how she had watched her own boys play the same games in another place, once-upon-a time.

CHAPTER TWENTY-FIVE
Changing Times

Nursing—the nursing she knew—was changing before Alice's very eyes. There had been signs of significant upheaval before the end of her training—the Salmon Report had been released in England foreshadowing not just the end of hospital rule by matrons, but also the rise of nurses above their hither-to subservient role as 'doctors' handmaidens'. And this was the beginning of nursing education moving to universities and colleges. It had happened in the USA and the UK, and was gaining momentum, so it was inevitable that it would happen in Australia. Some of the midwives Alice worked alongside were openly hostile to the ideas that were being implemented, arguing that there was no need to change the status quo—things worked quite well the way they were, they argued—but Alice quietly thought it could be a good thing to 'stir the pot' and give nurses the chance to advance themselves in the hospital system, if they were so inclined. She just hoped that the profession wouldn't lose the truly dedicated nurses, the ones who just lived to give a service to their patients, and their needs, and asked for nothing else.

Alice was uncertain about her own future in this new milieu. Her epaulettes and cap, which she wore proudly, were both to be made obsolete in the near future and there was talk of midwifery training also being transferred to universities. She talked her situation over with the matron—not the fiendish, fearsome matron of her training days, but a wise and thoughtful woman who had spent time in her early nursing career in the Aboriginal missions of the Northern Territory. She knew about life and nursing and recognised that nursing's transition to a science-based profession would be difficult, but she was convinced it would be a good thing in the long term. She suggested to Alice that she should apply for admission to a university course in Melbourne to convert her hospital qualification to an advanced-nursing degree because in the future a university qualification would be a requisite for any senior in-charge position in the hospital system. She could be a part-time student, the matron told her, and she could keep her position on the midwifery tutoring staff and better than that, she could complete her degree in two years because of her prior training. It sounded like a horrendous venture to Alice at first—certainly no adventure in wonderland for this Alice—but with no one else to consult, and no family commitments to hold her back, she applied to the university and was accepted for entry the following year. And it was hard; very hard. She often listened to her fellow students who had families and were holding down jobs as well, when they were gathered for lunch in the canteen, and their talk about their lives left her in awe of the way they not only managed to work and study too, but managed to stay sane! Alice finished her studies with good results, and with a grateful heart that it was at an end, she started to consider what else lay ahead for her.

Her graduation ceremony was due in two weeks' time, when she was notified through her Melbourne solicitor that the funds from the sale of the English house that had been her family home with Jack and their boys, had come through. This same solicitor had handled their divorce proceedings from the beginning and she had negotiated through him that Jack could keep the house and stay there until the boys' schooling was finished—but then it was to be sold. She hadn't thought anything about these sensitive matters for a long time and didn't find that the memories sat well with her when they were revived.

She had written about her early life in the stories that she typed in the peace of the library with the gardens just beyond the windows, and she would gaze outside searching for the right word or phrase to put to her memories to make sense of them—but she found that this prospect of another complicating issue in her life, and a resurgence of emotion from the abandonment she had once felt, was still raw. The stories that she had written were just for her—to clear her mind of troubling things from her past and to allow her to move on with her life, and here in the letter from the solicitor was everything she didn't want to remember, and it all came back to her with disturbing clarity.

She took leave of absence from her job after the graduation, and caught the overnight coach to Queensland to spend some time in the sun and make some decisions about the next stage in her life. It was a good thing for her to do: the solitude of her rented apartment on the fifth floor with its view of the beach and blue water behind it, and the glorious light that streamed through the windows day-in and day-out warmed her through and through, freeing her mind and helping her make order from the chaotic thoughts that shrouded her.

She stayed one week there, soaking up the sun and walking the sandy beaches before flying to Melbourne, and in the rain and cool wind of an August day she met a real estate agent, someone she had picked at random because she liked the look of her face in the newspaper advertisement. *Please show me any two-bedroom houses with character in a quiet street close to a shopping strip and a medical centre—and near a park*, she asked.

And she was shown just the house she knew she wanted—that very day. It had a white picket fence and a fruit tree in the small front garden which was overgrown with daisies. The back garden, accessed through the kitchen, had a steel-shed for storage and a little path that led to a laneway through a rotting timber gate. The shopping-strip (The Strip), that Alice had in her mind's eye, was there—just there as she had hoped, at the end of the lane. The rooms of the little house weren't large and they had old, disused Victorian fireplaces in each, but there was good light through the tall sash-hung windows in every room. She loved this house at first sight, but when the next-door neighbour lifted her head up from her garden-bed with her trowel still in her hand and said, '*Hello*' with such a welcoming smile and friendly voice, Alice had no doubt about her decision. She paid a deposit that afternoon, sitting in the agent's office in the shopping strip, and her heart felt so happy that she didn't understand what the feeling was at first.

Settlement on the house was very straightforward and completed within a month and it all happened so quickly that Alice wasn't ready—she still had her position at the hospital to consider—and she talked to the agents about letting it out on her behalf for the remainder of the year. The rental agreement stretched till after Christmas… and then till after Easter the following year… and then until the following Christmas. Alice thought often about how she wanted to be there in that house, (*her* house), but she delayed as long as someone was looking after it—and they *were* looking after it very well. They were a young, just-married couple when they moved in with the barest of furniture and no responsibilities; then they had a young baby, and then the baby became a toddler and then there was another baby on the way and they gave notice of their intention to vacate the house in the following New Year.

Alice by this time had taken up a position as a charge-nurse on a surgical ward at her hospital and was comfortable in her role there. She had very good staff and was able to implement changes and use the ideas and management theory she had studied in her degree course. She had lived alone for some years and happily so, and sought nothing else in her life. And then Kelly found her and changed her life until she lost him again and he left her forever.

CHAPTER TWENTY-SIX
Getting There

Alice had not given a name to Jack's boys when she wrote about them in her stories—they were just, *theirs, hers, his*. She had written cards to them at Christmases and on birthdays which she had never posted after they had come, on her invitation, to the commitment ceremony between her and Kelly in the back garden of her Melbourne house. She had not seen them since that day nearly twenty years before when she had proudly introduced them to Kelly, and Effie and her family, and she had taken the boys and their young children next door to see the new kitten. Her hairdresser with her kindly husband came to toast them that day, along with some of the other traders from The Strip that she had become close to, and a few of the friends she had made in Bendigo travelled down to celebrate with her too. On that happy occasion she had used her son's names, (*not his sons, her sons, their sons*) but their real birth names—to introduce them to everyone. These carefully chosen names were the names that she once had fretted over with Jack, tossing around possibilities from a book of names and their meanings in alphabetical order, late into the night before each was born. '*Too English', 'too easily shortened', too this, too that*, they said. *Names are so important*! Alice stated firmly. And in the days when they could joke together about such things, they began to introduce ridiculous names to the list and laughed about them. They also included some girls' names, but for some inexplicable reason they never thought for one moment that they would have a daughter. Alice's vision of motherhood for her, only raised pictures of sons, and as ultrasound scans were not de-rigueur in those days, they had no way of finding out a baby's gender for sure until they were here in the world, safely delivered by the midwife into the arms of their waiting mother. So, Alice took a notebook of favourite boys' names with her into the labour-ward to talk to Jack about when he was allowed to visit, to see what suited their baby best. They eventually settled on *Caleb,* meaning *'faithful and wholehearted'* for their first born, and saved *Finn*, meaning *'fair or white',* for their second son. As it turned out, both could have been called *Caleb*—if name meanings mean anything, (*Alice* for instance, meant *'noble and fair'* she read, and she didn't think that suited her at all). Finn was dark haired, and Caleb was the blond and fair one, but both boys were faithful and wholehearted which fitted them perfectly. Both were beautiful boys, both were intelligent and caring, energetic and sporting and they both made good careers for themselves—and resiliently stuck with their father, cared for him and made him happy, giving him grandchildren to enjoy with his partner at family gatherings and at all the special times in the calendar. *And they were worthy of a better Mother than I ever was to them*—Alice wrote in her notebook.

Jack had died of a stroke, she was actually very sad to read in a letter from her solicitor, a couple of years after Kelly died. He had left everything to his sons including the house that he had re-bought from Alice, paying her half out to her in a fair arrangement with their solicitor's help, after his young partner (of Dubai days), had left him to pursue her own academic life in Glasgow.

Alice sometimes thought that she had too much 'insider

knowledge', and when she heard of Jack's stroke, she found herself wondering what had gone amiss in his world that put him in line for such a devastating thing to happen. He had always prided himself on his fitness; he played the sports his young sons did—tennis, soccer, squash—and ran or walked long distances every day; and she was always hard-pressed to get him to eat butter and cheese and full-cream milk in their years together, and she had noticed that when the Danish girl came into his life, he had stopped eating meat. Perhaps that was the problem, she said to herself, not enough meat, only half believing it to be the truth, and in a wry jest with herself.

Alice retrieved the cardboard box containing her green velvet dress, wrapped loosely in white tissue paper, from the bottom of the hall cupboard, took it out and lovingly placed it on the bed, smoothing the nap and straightening the collar. *This needs dry-cleaning,* she told herself. Then she placed all the signed and addressed—but never posted—cards from her collection, into the empty box. Next, she collected the photographs from travels that were so very special to her—the photos that said something about the years she spent with Kelly. Many of their travels had been captured on their mobile phones and they had never bothered to have them all printed but some they had singled out to be processed as hard-copies, and these were the ones she had saved. She placed them all into separate manilla-envelopes writing carefully on the front with her Artline pen, some notes about each trip. To the photos she added the few of the boys, that she had with her in her purse, when she left Dubai and from the last time, she had seen them with their children socialising in her garden and playing with Effie's kitten. On top of the photographs in the box she placed coloured folders containing her short stories. There was her favourite story about the exquisite butterflies outside the window in the library in Bendigo, and another about the effect on the world if the sun suddenly disappeared—if the sun just failed to rise one day and thereby made humanity extinct. There were so many other stories that she had written from imagination, using the prompts that she saw around her—the activities of daily life of the people she saw on her travels and from her seat on the park bench, that stirred her mind's eye. She had edited and rewritten some of them and these she printed off from her computer using Kelly's beautiful printer (which was far too expensive to purchase, as she had pointed out to him at the time, he bought it). Many of her photos she sorted chronologically and downloaded onto a memory stick which she stapled to a story-folder with a thin ribbon. Kelly had taught her well how to do these things proficiently, and with confidence and ease—and she was so glad of that; in hindsight she was so very grateful to him for many things. But now she was tired and she slept in her familiar chair until the light began to fade and then she roused herself and went outside into her garden to see the end of the day, with just enough sunlight left to warm her face and make her smile.

The following day was Tuesday, she saw on her calendar on the fridge, and this was Edna's day. Edna used to come fortnightly to 'do' for her, but now she came weekly. Alice had refused any assistance from the council that she was eligible to receive at her age but because she had been granted a small government pension to supplement her superannuation money, she preferred to employ her own help in the house—someone who would move rugs and empty fridges and clean windows inside if asked, which was the really what Alice needed. Edna would change her bed sheets too, and this Tuesday was the day for that; there was system and order in the days of the week and the things that happened, and what she could expect which pleased Alice, and made her days easier. Edna, she thought, would be happy that Alice had sorted her fridge and relieved her of at least one of her chores, so today she could change the sheets and then start on the windows. Edna was fit and agile enough to be able to climb a step-ladder safely so Alice left her to her tasks while she continued sorting her papers and kept herself busy until Edna left to go to her next job along the street. Edna could let herself in with her own key, which was a bonus, so that Alice didn't have to be at home when she came and went. If the weather was good Alice would often use this opportunity to go and sit in her park and watch the ducks and quietly observe the walkers, some strolling filling in time, some brisk and passing through, not noticing the beauty of the trees and gardens, and there were often families she could watch having picnics on the grass on rugs spread around them. She had the dispassionate eye of a creator, a painter of scenes, an observer of life, taking in the colours and noises and smells as she had always done, in many different places and countries, and at different times in her life. She always found something she could write about and had from time to time wished she could sketch too, to enhance her stories. But just now she was done with her tales from the vignettes of her life—she had to finish her long-story soon—so she took no heed of this glorious morning to go and visit her park and instead she stayed home and, once Edna had gone—taking her money that Alice had placed in an envelope, from the hall table—Alice picked up her notebook and wrote ideas, headings, phrases, to make order of the complete story of her life and her plans. She set up her laptop in the un-used bedroom (*their* bedroom she still called it), the one with Kelly's clothes hanging in the wardrobe and the bed still made up as if waiting him to climb-in and warm the sheets for her. She sensed that she smelled him still, it was fanciful she knew—and really not possible—but that was what she thought. His clothes were still there and although they no longer smelled of cigarettes, they always had his own personal, and somehow comforting smell in their fibres—or so she wanted to imagine.

CHAPTER TWENTY-SEVEN
With Dignity

There was a time in Alice's life when she was fully engaged with birth, and birthing, and everything to do with that process of bringing life into the world, but still sometimes she met death and was shocked into the reality of the fickleness of the life-cycle, and then she became engaged in wanting to see life go out of the world with dignity. She cared for women and their partners whose expected and anticipated baby did not make it to the end of a term pregnancy, or if they did, their baby did not survive the birthing process or, as sometimes happened, they were too disfigured, too genetically malformed, to exist out of utero. And Alice began to consider life and death from a different point of view. She came to recognise that it would be good to have options: not in birth unfortunately—there were few options there, even though mothers might chose an active birth, or minimal intervention or a drug-free birth; a foetus can't choose its parents nor its parents' life-style—it is what it is, and mostly pre-determined at the moment of conception, Alice knew this; however, she reasoned often to herself: there could be a choice at the other end of a life which shouldn't be determined by old age, or deformity, but by choice at any point in a conscious life and she wanted to learn what more there was to know—what had already been discussed, what papers had been written about the subject—and her thinking became changed in the process of her discovery.

When she had been completing her advanced nursing degree, the students had been asked to write on the subject of euthanasia for the law component of the course. They would all have to present a ten-minute talk to their fellow scholars in the lecture theatre, at the microphone, they were instructed. Alice prepared her talk thoroughly. She researched on practices and beliefs across the world, and in different cultures, and wrote her paper well, bringing in that in years gone by, deformed babies would sometimes be smothered by their midwives and in some cultures these babies would be swaddled in cloth and left with the hippopotamus' in the river. She wrote about the problems encountered by countries trying to legislate for assisted suicide and the multitude of people who wanted to end their lives and were prohibited, by law, to do so. She had intended to conclude her talk with: '*In terms of life and death—the law is an ass*'.

She never did present what she knew would be contentious views that day; when it was nearly her turn to present at the lectern, she was so nervous that she felt physically sick, and left the lecture theatre to drive home early to the safety of her little house in Bendigo—in tears the entire way. That didn't mean that she was abandoning her thoughts and beliefs—they stayed with her for the remainder of her life, and she was a proud contributor to a film on physician-assisted dying that just fell short of what she saw as an almost ideal end to a life. The brave man who allowed himself to be filmed in his last days, decided in the end that he would not call on assistance and instead allowed himself to die over a longer time and with less dignity than an assisted death might have given him. But, there's the rub, Alice thought, everyone must make up their own mind about this; not be pressured or cajoled, but be prepared to use their own knowledge and desires to help fulfill their end-of-life wishes.

I went to bed with Doctor Rodney Symes one night and woke up enlightened, she thought to herself and laughed out loud at the thought... and the presumption... but there was no doubt that the residual effect of her night-time reading experience of his book *'Time to Die'* was life-changing in every way for her.

'Death could come about in any way and be controlled as one chose as long as a conscious decision was made—at the right time and place and confided in the right people', she read. But there was a problem here... what if the 'right' medical diagnosis for assisted dying wasn't available, or hadn't happened? What if one wasn't suffering from an incurable disease? What if one's condition wasn't terminal like breast or prostate cancer or a neurological condition like Parkinson's disease or motor-neurone disease, but instead just a debilitating and tragic condition like Alzheimer's, or cardiac failure, or, god-forbid, schizophrenia, or severe depression. It seemed to Alice that life-choices on death and dying were limited to chance events; chance diseases. She wasn't prepared to compromise herself and her hopes.

She had written her *Advance Directive*, leaving a copy at her doctor's, which stated very clearly that above all she did not want to have her dying sullied by the indignities—the ignominy—of death. That was what she feared most—that was what woke her in the night, those imprinted pictures in her mind of deaths that she had encountered of people obviously at the end of their days and in the process of dying; blood tests and other invasive procedures had confirmed that they were dying, but they had still been tortured with the insertion of urinary catheters (just to calculate their output on a chart) and intravenous fluid therapy (just to keep them hydrated). She had seen so many admissions from nursing homes—which were once considered 'God's waiting rooms', but in the middle of the night, when staffing was sparse, suddenly became the wrong place for the dying-elderly to be looked after with kindness and care and with people they knew around them. This is all that she didn't want for herself or for anyone else, really, but mostly for herself; she couldn't and wouldn't speak for anyone but herself. She had heard so many patients say to her that they had had enough of life and they wanted to end it all now and she was not ever in any position to help them and could just report what they said to the doctors who were there to be their 'advocates', she thought—but they merely ordered another medication to relieve any overt symptoms. *Dying would relieve their symptoms*, she screamed in her head so many times, but she was a good, obedient nurse and did exactly what she was told. But when her own time came, she knew she would be over and above obedience to anyone.

She spoke to groups of like-minded people whenever she could—gradually losing her anxiety about public speaking because she was so impassioned by her topic—and bored her guests almost to death at dinner parties and social gathering by espousing this philosophy. She just knew that *dying with dignity* was what she wanted for anyone and everyone. And, for herself.

When it was clear to her that her life was on the wane and she was in her own life's autumn season, she set about her plan with great conviction. She planned to achieve her goal with the minimum of distress to others. She had been alone for many years, never needing to call on anyone to help her until recently, but as a solitary person she was not just resilient but also resourceful. She was well aware of whom she could rely on, who would help and who would not, and decided quite early in her plans that her doctor was not one of those whose shoulders would support her—he would be full of ideas about the next strategy they could employ, anything to keep her alive; he would refer her to specialists who tested and prodded and prescribed medications that she would find difficult to swallow and she would view their treatments sceptically unconvinced that they would be of any benefit to her.

To be led down this track of the medicalisation of old-age would require frequent visits to her doctor's soulless office for repeat prescriptions and perfunctory examinations and there she would see the pictures of his long-suffering wife (Alice was convinced she was long-suffering although she had no proof), with his two children, taken years ago she decided, on his pristine desk, and she would be in despair as he paid an untold amount of attention to the computer screen in front of him and scarcely glanced at her. He would not see that she had dressed herself well for the visit, with polished shoes which matched her coat, tinted moisturiser on her pale face and pink colour on her lips (which she always thought more becoming than red for her at her age). *He has no compassion, no understanding of me at this stage in my life,* she ranted to herself on the way home from any visit— *he doesn't see that I am NOT a silly old woman—I am as much my own person as I have always been in my life, and especially now that I am at the end of it!* On her way home from her last appointment a month ago, she added to herself: W*ell, bugger him, then!*

Effie, her dear friend and neighbour Effie, was another matter. She was too close, too much of a regular visitor to her house, to be oblivious to the changes in Alice—the ankle swelling where a finger imprint stayed far too long and the effort involved in her day-to-day activities—but she would not want her to intervene and did not want to her to be involved in her plans. So, with the thorough planning of an experienced and frequent traveller, she began her preparations for her final destination.

She kept her appointment with her hairdresser and before making her slow walk home she picked up her green-dress from the dry-cleaners. She had taken to using Kelly's old walking stick which he had needed to use in his last few weeks, taking it with her on her little outings. Zoe, her hair-dresser commented that she had never seen her use it before and Alice told her that her foot was sore but there was no problem, she would get it checked by the podiatrist, and then they talked about the latest movie-star gossip, and what was happening in the area, the renewal of the park's play-equipment that the council was about to start, and when Alice left her in a pleasant mist of hair-spray, they hugged as they often did, but Alice felt a prickle of unfamiliar tears begin and covered the moment by asking to book a date for her next visit in a month's time. '*See you soon!*' she said, and waved as she passed in front of the shop window. '*Goodbye, Zoe Thank you,*' she added quietly to herself.

Alice was always a planner, a considerer of alternatives, a lateral thinker, and she rarely shared her plans until they were entirely complete—and she was not going to share her plans now.

She arranged for Effie's son-in-law George, to come and tidy the garden for her on Thursday that week, to trim the wild looking Photinia hedge, and remove the weeds in the path and re-mulch the garden beds. Kelly and Alice had planned the garden well: it thrived and looked interesting regardless of the amount of attention, or neglect, they paid it—provided that it was watered and pruned in season as needed—and together they took so much pleasure from it. While George was busy outside, Alice prepared her house. She went outside to give George his money in an envelope and asked him if he wouldn't mind leaving through the back gate into the laneway so she could have her little afternoon-nap undisturbed.

Alice tidied her bedroom, straightened the bed-spread and plumped the pillows and then removed the bundle wrapped in brown paper from the bedside table and took it with her into the living room. She placed the contents of the bundle on the little table beside her chair with a small jug of water, a damp face-washer, a folded cotton hand-towel and her mobile phone, then she switched on the table lamp before partially closing the louvres on the shutters against the afternoon sun.

Her laptop was still on the desk in the bedroom—the bedroom she had shared with Kelly—and she made sure it was fully charged before turning it off, shutting the lid on her stories on the desktop. The day before, she had printed-off the last of her pages and placed them in the box with the rest of her manuscript, along with the photos she had saved, and all the cards that she had never posted.

She went slowly to the bathroom and carefully washed herself in the walk-in shower stall that they had installed to make things easier for her to assist Kelly in his last days, and then she dressed herself in her green velvet dress with only a satin slip underneath and a pair of newly acquired Tena pants (no chemist was going to ask an old lady why she needed those, and no one did!). She cleaned her teeth (teeth worn-down now and discoloured, but still all her own), wiping the sink and bench top afterwards, and then went to the kitchen to make sure that George had left the garden as they had agreed. The French doors were still ajar a little, letting in an early evening breeze and she stood for a while looking out onto the patio and the garden beds beyond and felt calmed and thankful for the order that George had left behind him.

The pink camelias were in bloom still—the autumn winds would come soon and blow their petals into mounds under the wide door frame. '*My favourite time of year*', she spoke aloud, knowing this to be true. Autumn, which brought a gentle warmth to the air, and colour changes to the shrubs and trees of her garden: this place that she saw so vividly in her mind's eye where she had often sat with Kelly in peace and companionship sipping wine, before they were driven inside by the cool of the evening to then sit and read by the open-fire and discuss their day. She found her secateurs on the garden chair where she had left them two weeks before and she cut some late camelias to take indoors—short lengths which she placed in a vase on her sitting room mantelpiece without water.

Alice was at peace. She returned to the bathroom to put on her make-up—simple and tasteful as always with just a little pink lipstick to suit her dress colour—and retrieved her plain silver ring from the bench, the ring that that Kelly had given her—and put it on her left ring finger—she had always worn it on her right hand and although she had given the gesture no previous thought, it felt perfectly right for her to wear it as a married, committed woman at last. She sprayed the air with her favourite *Je Reviens* perfume and walked through it on her way out of the bathroom.

She was nearly ready. She checked the front door, leaving it locked but not chained, and came to sit in her old chair; testing its position for access to her side table and its contents. After Kelly left her and she was on her own she had moved the chair closer to the fireplace and facing the door, where the light was still good, but not too bright—just bright enough to read and write by. But today she didn't need to read or write—she was done with all that.

She had saved what she would need over a long time,

although not consciously saving it for any reason at all, she saved it anyway, and she worried that some of it might be out of date and ineffective—but she must take that chance. When Kelly was in the advanced terminal stage of his cancer, he had been prescribed strong, liquid pain-relief, an opioid, for him to take orally until the time came when he would need injections of morphine to keep him comfortable—but he had needed very little of it as it happened, so Alice just kept it in their bedside table still in the chemist's brown paper bag. In her grief and distress after Kelly died, she had asked for a sedative from Dr John in The Strip, and later some sleeping pills from a random doctor in Queensland near where she was staying, which the compassionate GP had no hesitation in prescribing once she knew something of Alice's story—but soon Alice had decided that she didn't need any medication to keep her calm, nor to help her sleep; she would handle her grief in her own resilient way. She kept the unopened packs in their neat labelled boxes and later bundled them together with the bottles of morphine mixture. She also added the medication that she had been prescribed when she wrenched her knee while trying to right herself in a fall from her chair a few months before. She had all she would need, she told herself, and she was absolutely convinced it would be sufficient. She was not a big woman; her clothes from decades before still fit her well, she was pleased to note, so she was fairly certain that she wouldn't need to take very much of what she had for its desired effect.

 She knew that she might be nauseated when she started to take the tablets so she gave herself an egg-cup full of antacid mixture and came to sit in her chair and looked around her. Her living room had always given her pleasure: the light through the shutters filtered and threw shafts onto her walls at all times of the day; the curves and shine of the old fireplace and mantelpiece; the subtle colours of the fire-side chairs where she and Kelly would sit at the end of the day, facing each other, but each absorbed in their own books or thoughts.

She was peaceful now after her breathless effort to shower and dress herself, and now she felt serenely comfortable—almost joyful in the pleasure of reaching the end of her planning and dressed in her outfit and, shoeless, she placed her feet up on her stool. Slowly and meticulously, she began.

She took the morphine mixture to which she had added orange cordial first, sipping the mixture through a paper straw and then swallowed the first of the strong pain-killers. She started to gag for a moment, but rested her head against the back of her chair before continuing to take the cut-up pills from the China plate on her table. Alice had prepared well—she had everything that she needed close at hand, including the damp face-washer which she wiped her mouth with as the tablets started to take effect. She had thought that she might be incontinent of urine as she succumbed to the overwhelming tiredness that she was expecting, and in addition to her pads, she had placed a cushion covered in a hand-towel underneath her before she settled into her chair and sat and waited for the end.

She knew that she had said all she wanted to say to everyone she had something to say to; she had written all she wanted to write and left the evidence to be easily found in her box; she had prepared herself so anyone who found her would know that this wasn't some random act carried out in the depths of depression, but a death achieved with dignity and of her own volition, by her own hand and at her own time—and *in* her own time—neither too soon, nor waiting too long when she would be in distressingly advanced, untreated heart failure.

She became breathless and restless for a short while, and she knew her mouth was open in a deep snore, a wheeze, and she began to dream. She had vivid colourful dreams of running on sand and flying into a cloudless sky and the elation of escaping from whatever was pursuing her and she had a sensation of involuntary shuddering which was unrelated to feeling cold, she didn't feel cold, she felt hot, but she wasn't able to rouse herself sufficiently to reach her table to take another sedative—she was powerless to act on her intentions to do anything. And she felt herself sliding into oblivion, deep, deep oblivion.

EFFIE'S TALE

I am Effie; my mother was Italian and my father was Greek and he named me for my grandmother, Euphemia which means 'well-spoken' which I definitely am not, which is why I have asked Alice's sons to translate and transcribe this story for me and for you to read and know about Alice.

Alice knew about my origins, but always referred to me as *Australian/Italian* and I think because she was always so proud of being an Australian herself that it would never have occurred to her that it should have been said the other way around.

She never knew how much she was loved, how much she was admired by everyone who came in contact with her, for her beauty of face and beauty of being, her intelligence and the strength of her character. She was a wonderful, determined and resourceful woman. I knew this from the moment I set eyes on her when she came to see the house next door to us for the first time. I watched her through the hedge, as I had watched many people, couples mostly and far too many investors, who came to view the house which had been empty since its last owner—a Greek immigrant as it turned out—lived and died there. He died of old-age which seems a diagnosis that doesn't apply any more, it seems that everyone has to die of 'a cause', but pass away he did, quietly and with dignity with his family around him. Alice hated those words 'pass away', and other silly phrases applied to dying, but I would never use *pass away* disrespectfully; I have the same common-sense about death that she had, and that is probably one of the many things that we really liked about each other.

On the day I first saw Alice, she was bedraggled—her long fair hair wet against her head but she looked smart, wearing a red raincoat that contrasted with the white daisies in the front of the house and created a picture that seemed to say that she belonged there. It had been raining and windy since the morning and I had taken a chance in a break in the weather to start some gardening when she arrived. She could only have been in the house a few minutes before she came out with the pretty agent, a family friend of mine, behind her and for a moment, I thought yet again that a potential purchaser wasn't interested. And then she turned around and I saw her face, her shining eyes, tears maybe, or just a hint of them, and I knew that she would always be my friend and neighbour. I stood up and smiled at her and said '*hello*', as always, a little conscious of my accent with a stranger, but she smiled back at me and in her soft and gentle English voice said, '*Hello to you too; this is such a lovely house*'. She waved as she left in the agent's car and I went inside to tell Joe that I thought we might have a new neighbour soon.

It was some time before she actually came to live here, and that was with Kelly who had brought her peace and happiness, but in the meantime, I had the joy of knowing the little family that lived there. They took care of Alice's' house, and they nurtured, not just their family but the garden too and they created a life for themselves in the neighbourhood, shopping at our vegetable stall in The Strip and getting to know my own growing children, and our first old cat before he 'passed'! I also saw Alice from time to time when she was in Melbourne visiting friends, she would call in on the off-chance that I was home and then talk to me about everything on earth before she finally asked, '*How is it going next door?*' She would never be intrusive, not ask the agent to take her through the house, but from our talks I knew she had plans, things she wanted to replace, repair and install—like a French door from the kitchen to the back yard, (or the garden as she hoped it would be one day). And then she would be gone, back to Bendigo, leaving a faint hint from her perfume and a memory of a pleasant few hours spent with a warm and gentle friend.

I knew about Alice's writing and had read some of it, and some of her stories that made me laugh and admire her more, but I knew nothing about her last story that she worked so hard to complete, her chance to pull her life together in words and when I had the chance to read it, I understood why she had written it in another's voice—someone telling a story about someone else. She had said often after a couple of red wines at my dining table, that she was sick of writing about herself as *me, I, myself—in the first person,* because there was no freedom in that, to write that way she had to tell the truth, the painful un-mitigating truth (Finn said) of everything in her life and she had not ever wanted to do that, she would say on her third glass. And yet, I can see that there was so much truth in her story, but perhaps using a narrator gave her the sovereignty (that is Finn's word, not mine—I always thought sovereignty was to do with kings and queens but I can see that it fits in the story of Alice I am telling), but the word 'liberty' I know—so perhaps another's voice gave her the liberty to be honest with her feelings, her disappointments, her wishes and desires and in fact be totally honest with herself.

I never needed any of that from her. I never needed her to tell me about her life for me to love her, and that is why I did what I did.

The day I came to see her, using my key and surprising her

from a sleep in her chair, it was a surprise for me to see that she had hidden from me her increasing debility, her heart was giving up, she was sick I saw and her time was limited. Usually when I visited, she was dressed for the occasion and would put on her makeup and a little lipstick and for all intents and purposes looked like the same dear friend I had always known. I saw that she was really aging, as we both were, but she was becoming breathless, her legs were very swollen but she always had an excuse for these changes, covering her lack of mobility in some way or another. She was a fine actress and had nearly fooled me! The first indication that things were very wrong, was seeing the disorder of her house—she was never like that, order was the mainstay of her life (thank you Finn, I might have written that order was her strength), and always had been—and then I had the realisation that she had not walked out to visit her ducks in the park or shopped in The Strip for some time, relying on the meals that I brought to her when I cooked too much for my family or the frozen packs she asked Edna to pick up from the supermarket on her way to clean for her.

I visited her on that Monday afternoon and had the impression that she didn't want to extend my visit this time. If she had, she would have brought out one of Kelly's stored, dusty reds and opened it with flourish and a little drama, telling me about the vintage and when and where it was bought with the creativity of a skilled story-teller, but this day she was keen for me to go home.

Tuesday was Edna's day, so I stayed away and on Wednesday I knocked on Alice's door (she would have to get up and open the door if I didn't use my key, I thought). She was cheerful (a word Finn and I could both use about her), and welcoming—something seemed to have been resolved in her and she was not shifty at all. She told me she had been busy getting her papers in order and showed me how she had set up the laptop in the main bedroom and was going to get on with transcribing her written notes and stories onto the computer. I saw that her favourite green-velvet dress was laid out on the bed and we talked about how amazing it was that it still fit her in the body although I thought that the Cinderella collar would show how thin and wrinkled her neck was now. '*Didn't we have a lovely time that day when we had our commitment ceremony in the garden?*' she said. And I said, '*Yes*'. Nothing else needed to be said.

I made an appointment to see Dr John on Thursday morning, the first available day for him. He was still Alice's doctor though she actually had very little time for him—she avoided any check-ups, or requests for follow-ups from his clinic, and had often been outspoken about his lack of care and empathy when Kelly was dying. But he was still her doctor, which I always found strange—perhaps it was the familiarity and nearness of the clinic or maybe her reluctance to take personal issues elsewhere and tell her whole story all over again. She was always a very private person; she wasn't really shy but she lived a lot in her mind, which I think is one of the best things about her writing—you can read how her mind worked.

On Wednesday afternoon I called in to see Alice again, but this time I didn't use my key, I rang the bell and I could hear her calling to me that she was coming. It took her a while to get to the door; she said she had been sleeping although she didn't look as if she had been, but I was pleased that she was well enough to walk to the door and her voice sounded strong, although she was quite breathless from the effort. We sat outside in the back garden for a while first with a cup of tea and enjoying the afternoon sun.

She offered me a glass of wine that she always made sound like a health tonic—*a little glass to fortify us?* she would ask, her head on one side in the cheeky, questioning way she had sometimes. Her eyes looked tired, as if she hadn't slept for some time, but she still looked directly at me as we talked and when we were sitting her breath came more evenly and easily as we sipped our wine. I didn't tell her that I was going to see Dr John on Thursday; I would leave that till I had seen him. I needed to talk to him about Alice's health and I wasn't sure how she would take that. Anyone talking about her, or on her behalf, was something she thought of as a betrayal, she had told me once, but I cared too much for her not find out if there was anything I could do to help her. She would not want to go to hospital to be assessed, I knew that, but I was so concerned I had to share my worries with someone. I rang Caleb in England to talk things over.

I had met both her sons, and their families, at the commitment ceremony in the garden all those years ago, when Alice and Kelly were fit and active, in love and so very excited about the life ahead of them. I understood how the boys became estranged from their mother, (they had no need of each other, it seemed to me) and there were so many things that went on between her and their father before I met her, but I wrote letters to the boys anyway, without telling Alice, because I felt very close to them from the moment, I first met them, and I thought they should know about her. She would have told me I was interfering I know, but sometimes we have to do things that make us feel better too.

Dr John was amazing (Finn said I should say 'professional' or 'supportive', but *amazing* is the word that describes what he said and did!). He had as much understanding of Alice and her dying wishes as I had and he helped us make her last hours comfortable and just the way she would have wanted it all to be. He organised for an oxygen tank to be delivered quickly, and came to the house and… sorry, I have got ahead in my story, and Alice wouldn't have liked that.

I meant to say, that I used my door key to come in and see Alice on Friday morning and I was almost too late. She was sitting up on her old pink chair in the sitting room wearing her lovely green velvet dress with her black velvet shoes on the floor near her. Her feet were too puffy to put them on. She looked peaceful, as if she was soundly asleep, but there was vomit on her lips and down her dress. She was breathing gently and I could feel that her heart was still beating. I cleaned up her mouth and the front of her dress while I waited for Dr John, but I left the bottles and pills on the little table for him to see. He was so kind. He didn't seem to be at all surprised at what she had tried to do and explained to me that she would wake up soon and she would be very angry and disappointed that she hadn't been successful in her attempt to end her life *her* way, but he could make her comfortable, here in her home with all her things around her, and give her a little more time and chance to say goodbye properly. He also said that she could stay in her chair; her special chair, that she loved so much which had travelled across the world with her. We would need to help her use a commode when the diuretics took effect, he said, and he would arrange for a palliative care nurse to come to help. He stayed and sat beside her holding her hand until she started to wake up, unsure of where she was and when she realised, she cried out, and clung to Dr John, her eyes wide and afraid. I put the heater on in the room and opened the shutters fully to let in the light—and I felt useless, not knowing what to do to help.

Dr John gave her some morphia which he injected into the

top of her leg to help her breathing and help her relax, he said, and something to help drain the fluid from her heart—he explained everything he was doing to her, and when the boys arrived, he was there and talked gently with them in the kitchen, explaining that Alice had very little time left.

Joe picked the boys up from the airport while I stayed with Alice, and by the time they arrived Alice was awake and clearheaded and became very emotional when she saw them come into the room. She kept repeating '*my* boys, *my* boys!' and she hugged them and kissed them as they knelt beside her chair and there was so much love that I broke down and cried with them. Joe cried too, but in his manly way—wiping his eyes with his big handkerchief and then blowing his nose.

There was no need for words as we all sat around in that room, with filtered afternoon light from the window, there was no sense of waiting for something; we were just there spending time with Alice.

She woke and dozed, her breathing eased, and each time she woke she spoke to us: '*Boys, there is a box in my wardrobe—that's for you. Effie and Joe, you look after that cat, she's getting old too you know! Doctor John, thank you, I'm sorry I have been such a bother to you, but thank you for saving me for this, it's a better way—and I am happy.*' Finally, she said '*This is what I always wanted—to die surrounded by loved ones, my family and friends. I love you all. Thank you!*' And then, with Doctor John holding her hand, she died.

There was no funeral service for either Kelly or Alice; Alice didn't believe that was necessary and her wishes were respected. She had donated her body to the university for research and that was handled by the undertakers, and she wore her green dress to the end. We held a happy wake in her back garden before her boys went home to their families, and all her friends from The Strip and the hospital in Bendigo came, and Edna and Zoe too, and we raised a toast to her and told stories about her and there was lots of laughing. She loved to laugh; she would have been happy to know that this was a joyful occasion. Finn wanted to say that it was *heart-warming,* but Alice often used the word *joyful* to describe a time when she felt *happy*, so joyful stays!

Alice's house went on the market and there were several offers in no time at all, but in the end our oldest son bought it and moved in with his young family. Our second old cat died and we buried her behind the shed in Alice's garden which was a favourite spot for her to lie in the sun. And our lives went on, but we never, ever forgot Alice who had thought she was 'solitary and reclusive'—we read about that in her book that her boys got published for her, but in fact she wasn't really ever alone because we all thought so often about her, but she was her own person always, and as we had agreed at her wake: she was never just anybody. . she was Alice, and we loved her.

Caleb's Story

Finn says we each have a different view of our mother, and of the time she stayed behind and we flew away with our father to another world—another life in England—and I think he might be partly right. Finn is the writer; the deep-thinking, sensitive and creative one of us, like our mother, whereas I am rational, hands-on and practical and—to be honest—also like our mother. We each have traits inherited from her that have made our lives good and well-lived, and we are grateful to her for that. And I know we share memories of the time before *whatever happened* when she was warm and loving, teasing and laughed along with us, before we went to Dubai and before we were in our teens—this was the memory that brought us back to see her commit herself to Kelly in Australia so many years ago.

She looked so beautiful that day in the sunshine and glowing with the love she left for Kelly. We didn't like him very much. We said to ourselves that we could see through his charm, and poetic ways, and his manipulation of our mother—the way she financed their travel, allowed him to share her house with him and how he kept her away from us. But some of that was unfair. In our maturity we saw that if she had wanted to, she would have connected with us and our families but we also saw that the gap was too long, too full of angst, and in our youth, we belonged to Jack and Ingrid.

We always suspected that Kelly had another life in Vietnam, when he was a free-lance journalist—maybe he even had a family, we would say to each other privately. We didn't talk to our father about Alice, never raised any discussion about the why's and wherefores of their split, for a long time. And we had the distinct impression that his liaison with Ingrid was not initiated by him in the first place; Ingrid was an opportunist, saw a chance with Jack and took it and flew away with him—with us. When she eventually left our family home, just when it was about to be sold and the proceeds divided between our parents, we can't say we were sad for ourselves, although Jack took it hard—he had never had to cope on his own, make his own decisions, forge his own way, care for his own health and well-being—first there had been Alice and then Ingrid to take care of him. Ingrid, as a stepmother did her best with us but she pushed Jack into sending us to boarding-school (it would be *'best for their education'*, she told him), as weekly boarders of one of the better schools in the area. Great move, actually as it turned out—we came back to our house every weekend, but we were encouraged to write letters *'home'* during enforced time in the recreation hall every week, along with the other longer-term boarders. We didn't write our letters to *'home'*, we wrote them to our mother, and although she never got to read them because we never sent them to her, they served as a loving reminder to us about her and that she had been a significant person in our lives. We took our boyhood letters with us to Australia in our suitcases bound for Melbourne the first-and-only time we had visited there with our families. We left our letters with Effie on that visit—next door Effie, who was so much more than just a neighbour to our mother. We had an instant rapport with her and knew we could trust our letters to her with the proviso that she wasn't to give them to Mother unless Effie thought there was a time when she needed to read them. There never was a time, Effie told us, when Alice was in a maudlin or reflective mood when it would have been right to give them to her, so they had remained in the drawer of Effie's antique bureau, with its pull-down desk top, for all this time.

But the gift that Effie gave us instead was *her* letters to us over the years, filling us in with details of Mother's life, the way she had nursed Kelly and picked herself up out of the despair she felt when he was gone (*died*, Mother would have insisted!), and about her writing, and she sometimes included copies of applicable stories that Alice had shared with her. Mother was a beautiful writer, descriptive and often funny and we sometimes showed them to Jack after Ingrid had gone, and before he became unwell. At those times he would talk about our mother so fondly, remembering good times with her and remind us that he loved her very much which was why he had followed her to Australia so many, many years ago. When Jack (we called him Jack, not Dad), had a stroke and lost his mobility, we would go and visit him in the nursing home and read him Effie's letters and Mother's stories and he always seemed brighter when we left… unknowingly, through Effie, Mother had given herself to him in his last days and we loved her even more for that.

When we got the phone call that this was our last chance to see Alice before she died, there was no hesitation on our part— we booked the earliest flight we could for just the two of us. Joe would meet us at Melbourne airport and take us straight to the house, Effie told us.

The incredible thing was that she was still as beautiful as we remembered, she still glowed even in her dying, (or perhaps because of it, Finn said poetically), and we each talked to her, told her things we had wanted to say for a long time and she knew us, called us 'her boys', and told us things she had wanted to say for a long time too. We held her soft hands and saw that she had put her ring from Kelly onto her wedding finger and remembered that she had made a big point of having it placed on her right hand at the ceremony—the friendship finger she said. Perhaps now she finally thought that she had committed herself to Kelly sufficiently to justify calling herself married to him. There is no doubt that we both thought that too, but knowing how practical she was about so many things we knew there would be a reason for it and were not surprised when she took it off her finger and handed it to me to take to my daughter and tell her that the best gift you can give a person is not just friendship, it is a commitment in health and sickness to be there for them till the end.

Before she closed her eyes and died, she looked at us all gathered around her, in her faded pink-chair in her lovely room with light streaming through the shutters that Effie had opened for her, and she told us: *'This is what I always wanted—to die surrounded by family and loved ones. I love you all. Thank you!'*

We had no problem submitting Alice's manuscript posthumously to Finn's publisher who accepted it, un-edited, and published it for a small fee; *'It's a fine piece of work although not perfect—the heart and truth of it will help it sell'*, he said. But we were not interested in post-publication sales as Alice would not have been; we just wanted to have a book in her memory that she would have been proud of—and on her behalf, we were proud too.

There was nothing prosaic about our Mother, Alice McPhee—indeed not, we agreed—and so it was simple to find a title for her book that said it all: Alice was *Never Just Anybody... and Never Just a Nurse!*

Epilogue

It took some time for him to tell us, but Doctor John knew our mother when she was a young student nurse when he was encouraging the use of honey as a treatment for bedsores as a resident at her training hospital. He never told our mother that he remembered her when she came to see him at his practice when her partner Kelly was so ill, and he never would. He couldn't tell her that he had loved her for such a very long time either, it was against his principles to do so, but I can see now that the tenderness he showed to her when she was dying was love in its purest form.

He found love for himself when he least expected it, and he found a family after many missed chances too, and then he wrote about his life. I know this because after he had read our mother's story which we shared with him after she died, he wrote and asked me if I could help him publish his story as a legacy to Alice and for what she had inspired him to do for others.

He titled it: '*Go Gently, Sandpiper...*'. Alice was his sandpiper... and he is Doctor John Barwick.

I am Finn Ryan, and I am so proud and pleased to be able to do that for him through my agent, and Caleb and I we are very grateful to him for his part in our mother's last days and for his part in our lives.